"Look out!"

"Get down," Flynn shouted. Another loud bang cracked through the air and the aircraft dipped precariously.

A buzzer sounded and a couple of lights flashed from the dashboard of the helicopter. Derek responded immediately by turning the aircraft away from the shooters.

Another bullet ripped into the back of the helicopter, and a plume of smoke began pouring from the engine.

"We've been hit," he said over and over again into his microphone as he tried to transmit their location and the call numbers.

Another gust of wind took them higher, and he could tell that he was fast losing control of the aircraft. His speed increased, and smoke, burning smells and heat permeated the cabin.

His entire engine was on fire. The heat in the cabin was almost unbearable.

Derek kept shouting into his headset, but there was no response from the tower. He tried one last time.

"Mayday, Mayday. We're going down!"

Kathleen Tailer is a senior attorney II who works for the Supreme Court of Florida in the office of the state courts administrator. She graduated from Florida State University College of Law after earning her BA from the University of New Mexico. She and her husband have eight children, five of whom they adopted from the state of Florida. She enjoys photography and playing drums on the worship team at Calvary Chapel in Thomasville, Georgia.

Books by Kathleen Tailer

Love Inspired Suspense

Visit the Author Profile page at LoveInspired.com.

Showdown in the Rockies

KATHLEEN TAILER

LOVE INSPIRED SUSPENSE
INSPIRATIONAL ROMANCE

LOVE INSPIRED® SUSPENSE
INSPIRATIONAL ROMANCE

ISBN-13: 978-1-335-98005-2

Showdown in the Rockies

Copyright © 2024 by Kathleen Tailer

For questions and comments about the quality of this book, please contact us at CustomerService@Harlequin.com.

® is a trademark of Harlequin Enterprises ULC.

Love Inspired
22 Adelaide St. West, 41st Floor
Toronto, Ontario M5H 4E3, Canada
www.LoveInspired.com

Printed in Lithuania

Recycling programs for this product may not exist in your area.

MIX
Paper | Supporting responsible forestry
FSC® C021394

My brethren, count it all joy when ye fall into
divers temptations; Knowing this,
that the trying of your faith worketh patience.
But let patience have her perfect work,
that ye may be perfect and entire, wanting nothing.
—*James* 1:2–4

For our wonderful family at Engage Church in Tallahassee, our missionary friends in Africa and Israel, and our incredible neighbors in Shell Point, Florida. Thank you all for your kindness, forbearance and unwavering love.

A special thank-you to Mike McElroy for his technical expertise. Any mistakes are truly my own.

I continue to be blessed and thankful for my wonderful family: Jim, James, Bethany, Daniel, Keandra, Jeremy, Jessica, Nathan, Anna, Megan, Joshua O., Bradley, Brayden and B.J. Also, in loving memory of our son, Joshua Evan Tailer, who will forever be in our hearts.

ONE

The man was dead.

His bare hand reached out and pointed awkwardly toward the tree line, the fingers curled as if grasping for something just beyond his reach. Blood was splattered on the snow around his body…*so much blood.*

An icy chill swept down Flynn Denning's spine as she refocused her camera. She had seen dead bodies before—unfortunately—at her new job as a detective in Tallahassee, Florida, but the horrific scene below still made her stomach twist into knots as the helicopter she was in flew over the unexpected and grisly sight. She wondered fleetingly if she would ever get used to seeing death displayed in such a macabre tableau. The bright snow contrasted with the dark red stains that covered a substantial part of the clearing. She hadn't known what to expect when she'd found the map of the Colorado Rockies and notes in her sister's house. The handwritten remarks were vague and mentioned a company named Bear Creek Vacation Rentals and a possible meth lab, but not much else. Flynn hoped that the notes and map had something to do with why her only sister, Erin, was now fighting for her life in the nearby hospital. Erin had been shot in the abdomen three days ago by an unknown perpetrator and still hadn't regained consciousness due to massive blood loss.

Flynn knew from the notes that her sister had been investigating a local drug cartel, but she had few details. Erin was also a detective, but she was employed by the local police department in the small town of Frisco, Colorado, and when Flynn had asked about the cases Erin was working on, the local force had been unable to link any of them to her sister's shooting. In fact, according to Erin's captain, they didn't have a single lead. They were digging into some of her past arrests, but so far, nothing had panned out.

The local team also knew nothing about Erin's drug cartel investigation, so Flynn had decided to take the bull by the horns and investigate the case herself—even if she did have only Erin's chaotic notes and a map to go by. She had to do something while her sister was lying in the ICU fighting for her life. Flynn had never been good at waiting for things to happen. She was a woman of action, and sitting around, hoping the local police force would catch Erin's shooter while she twiddled her thumbs, just wasn't going to work for her. Still, Erin had clearly been in the beginning phases of her investigation—her notes gave coordinates and vague hints, but nothing concrete. Apparently Erin had participated in a drug bust in Frisco, and one of the men she'd arrested had tried to secretly bargain his way out of a prison sentence by revealing more about the drug operation. When the attempt failed, the suspect later denied he had tried to make a deal, but Erin was good at her job, and had evidently started investigating his claims on her own.

Flynn hadn't expected to find much on this helicopter trip, but now, after seeing the grisly scene below, she was sure that Erin had been on the right track.

Flynn glanced back out the helicopter window and snapped a few more photos. Why was a dead body way out here in the middle of nowhere, slowly being buried by the snow in the remote Rocky Mountains? How did the scene below tie into the drug cartel? Questions spun in her head. Flynn shifted slightly in the helicopter seat so she could determine the exact cause of death, but no matter what angle she chose, it didn't help.

She focused her camera on the snow and followed the dark streaks of red that marred the wintry scene. Maybe, just maybe, her photos could help local law enforcement figure out what had happened. She was well out of her jurisdiction, but she was still a skilled investigator, and she wanted to help however she could. If she came to them with real evidence, maybe it would lead to the arrest of whoever shot her sister.

She leaned forward, adjusting as the helicopter turned. They had come to another nearby clearing, about the size of a baseball field, circled with aspens and pines. They helicopter hovered about eighty feet over the snow, and Flynn grimaced at the sight.

There was more than one body.

"Do you see that, Derek?" She turned toward the pilot who was flying them over the area and pointed.

"Unfortunately, I do," he said tightly. Even through the metallic speakers on the headset, she could hear a protective edge in his voice. "We're right over the coordinates you provided from that map you showed me. Is this what you expected to find?"

Flynn met his eyes for a moment, then shook her head. "My sister's notes were pretty vague. I wasn't sure what to expect, but it definitely wasn't this."

"What's going on?" Flynn's eleven-year-old nephew, Kevin, pushed forward from the back of the helicopter, trying to get a better view out the window. "What do you see? Is there something weird out there?" Instead of the ominous tones she'd heard from their pilot, Kevin's voice sounded more interested than he'd been in anything else they'd talked about today...or all week. According to Erin, Kevin had been struggling ever since his father had abandoned him and Erin over a year before. The boy had been sullen and moody. Flynn and Erin had discussed Kevin quite a bit over the phone, but now that Flynn was actually in Colorado and had been taking care of the youth while Erin was in the hospital, she was seeing his behavior in person for the first time since his father's unexpected departure. Counselors hadn't been able to help him so far. And now that his mother's life was in jeopardy, Flynn was worried that his emotional state was only going to worsen. On top everything he had already been struggling with, he had to be terrified that he might become an orphan, even if he was desperately trying not to show his fear.

A wave of regret swept over her. She wouldn't have brought Kevin with them if she'd known they'd find a murder scene up here. Surely he didn't need to be exposed to something so hideous. The boy had been so obstinate and difficult in the hospital, though, that she'd thought the helicopter ride would be a good distraction for him. Flynn had also hoped that during the trip, she would learn a clue or two about who had tried to murder her sister. Still, the scene below was nothing like she'd expected, and she wished she'd left Kevin with a friend back in Frisco.

She turned to the boy and chose her words carefully, not wanting to add to the boy's trauma. "Some people have been killed," Flynn said gently. "You don't want to see it. There's a crime scene down there."

"A crime scene? Here?" Kevin's voice showed his surprise, and when Flynn looked over at him, he looked a bit paler than before. "What happened? Can you tell?"

Derek turned but didn't answer the boy. He looked back at Flynn. "I count three. Is that what you see?"

"Yes," she replied. "Kevin, try not to look. I'm going to take a few more pictures for the police, and then we need to go back to Frisco and take my SD card to the authorities. They'll have to send a team up here to investigate." She snapped several more photos as Derek banked the helicopter and turned so she could photograph a different angle.

"Good grief. It looks like a war zone down there," Derek muttered, pulling her back out of her thoughts and into the here and now. "The victims were shot, that much is clear."

Now that they were closer, the manner of death was much more apparent. "You're right," Flynn agreed. "At first, I was afraid maybe a wild animal had gotten them." She paused. "I only made detective a few months ago, so I'm still learning. Did you come across scenes like this very often in the military?"

"Unfortunately," Derek said under his breath. Even though he had murmured the comment, the word still went through the headset loud enough for Flynn to hear the desolation in his voice.

She looked back at the scene below them. A copious amount of snow was pink or red near the bodies, and now that they were closer, it appeared that the victims had been trying to escape and had been shot in the back. Footprints from the attackers came from behind and then circled each of the victims. Two were wearing winter clothing, so it was hard to determine their race or even their sex, though by their size they all seemed to be adults. The first body she had noticed was dressed in jeans and a red-and-black flannel shirt. He appeared to be an adult male, with short-cropped black hair, but it was difficult to be sure.

Flynn turned her camera to a couple of buildings on the side of the clearing and nestled into the edge of the surrounding woods. There was a large log cabin–style house that had obviously seen better days. The structure looked abandoned and leaned slightly to the left. Several shingles were missing, and paint peeled from various spots on the dark wooden walls. The building was situated closer to the other side of the tree line and stood about a hundred yards away from where the bodies lay in the snow. There was also a pole barn with an attached structure farther down the valley, and something that could have served as a helicopter pad near the house in the middle of the field. The pole barn housed some sort of equipment, a large tractor and a host of other items including a broken-down truck that had obviously been there for quite some time. A couple of snowmobiles were parked near the house's front door, but they had a few inches of snow on them, as if they hadn't been driven in the last couple of days.

"What is this place?" Flynn breathed almost to herself.

"An abandoned home turned meth lab, if I had to guess," Derek responded. "Do you smell that?"

"Smells like cat pee," Kevin volunteered.

Flynn wrinkled her nose and shook her head. She had never spent much time around young boys, but one thing she knew without a doubt—Kevin seemed to have a fascination with nasty smells.

"That's ammonia," Derek confirmed. "The smell gives it away. Ammonia is one of the key ingredients for making methamphetamine. We came across a few meth labs in Iraq, and I recognize the smell. We need to get out of here. Labs can be really dangerous. If the cooks don't do everything perfectly, the whole building can explode. Not to mention the fact that three people were murdered down there and the shooters are probably still hanging around." He pointed at the cabin. "I see some smoke coming out of that chimney. We are not alone."

"I agree. Let's get out of here," Flynn said as she sat back in the seat. Had her sister known about this meth lab? Had the drug dealers shot Erin before she could investigate further and shut the lab down? Questions plagued her mind.

"How long were you in the army?" Kevin suddenly asked, leaning closer to the pilot.

Derek turned his head as he steered the helicopter and took a moment to respond. "Eight years."

"That's so cool," Kevin opined. "Where were you stationed?"

"I did three tours," Derek confirmed.

"What did you do over there?" Kevin asked, apparently unable to keep the enthusiasm out of his voice.

"I flew Boeing AH-64 Apache helicopters in the sandbox—mostly in Iraq," Derek answered tightly.

"Man, that is so awesome! Why did you get out? Flying for the army sure sounds like more fun than flying around these mountains all day for the tourists. This is probably the most excitement you've ever had in Colorado."

Derek pursed his lips and didn't answer. Flynn glanced at him expectantly, but it was clear from the look on his face that they had broached an area that he had absolutely no desire to discuss. Flynn hadn't seen Derek King since their college days, and she'd truly been surprised when they had arrived at the airport and seen him running the flight check on the helicopter. She had spoken with a female receptionist to make the reservation and had no idea King Helicopter Tours was owned and operated by her old boyfriend. Back in college, she and Derek had dated for almost three years before they graduated. They had even talked about marriage, but then Derek had suddenly broken up with her and joined the army, with very little explanation. The breakup had been brutal, and Flynn hadn't heard from him since. In her mind, the wedge between them had all boiled down to one central truth—he had chosen a military career over marrying her, and once he'd made the decision, he hadn't been able to get away from her fast enough.

She had eventually forgiven him and tried to move on, but seeing him again brought feelings back that she thought she had resolved long ago, and the knot that formed in her stomach every time he glanced at her told her she hadn't quite gotten him out of her system yet after all.

She eyed him carefully. He was bigger now, had filled out quite a bit during his time in the military. His shoulders were broad and muscular, and his arms and legs were equally well-built and strong. He still wore his dark brown hair in a short style, and his handsome face had a few new lines of maturity and stress that only made him more attractive. He was also wearing a well-trimmed beard and mustache and looked the part of a mountain man instead of the former military aviator she knew him to be. His carefree swagger was gone, though, and he now moved with that military bearing that people outside the service could never quite duplicate. The posture was like a confidence that never wavered, no matter the circumstance.

She had to admit, even though eight years had passed, he was still one very good-looking man. His bold, rugged features and firm cheekbones lent him an air of authority. She also liked the way his dark blue eyes captured everything around him. She paused, thinking back to the last time she'd seen him. Despite their horrible breakup and the way he had so callously thrown their relationship away, she had still always remembered him as a fun and gregarious person. The man she had encountered today, however, was serious and subdued. She wondered at the change in him. Anyone who'd served in the military and seen action probably had horror stories replay in their mind from time to time. Maybe Derek had experienced a horrible event while on active duty that had turned him into this sullen and tight-lipped man. Or had there been something else in his personal life that had changed him? There was no ring on his finger, but from his current expression, it was clear she wasn't about to find out any of the missing details from his life. He seemed professional but also distant, as if he were somehow living in a shell, bricked off from the rest of the world.

She turned away and made an effort to study the landscape. Attractive or not, she knew instinctively she would never pursue any sort of relationship with Derek King ever again. She was done with relationships and men, and once her sister had recovered, she would be returning to Florida on the first available flight. Until then, taking care of her nephew and finding out who shot her sister were her only priorities. That was more than enough to keep her busy. She didn't need or want to give Derek King a second chance to break her heart.

Derek subtly shook his head as he piloted the helicopter. He was glad the kid was interested in the military. Despite the negatives, like losing friends and family during wartime, he truly appreciated people who wanted to serve their country. Still, he didn't talk about the army— not with anyone. They had trained him to fly during his initial entry rotary wing training at the US Army Aviation Center of Excellence at Fort Novosel, Alabama. After his third tour had ended in a devastating crash, he had gotten out early with an honorable discharge from his thirteen-year commitment and taken his piloting skills to the civilian world. That expertise was all he wanted to remember from his time in the service. The other memories were too painful to dwell on.

Flynn apparently picked up on his reticence and changed the subject before he had to come up with an answer to Kevin's question. "Did you note the coordinates of that meth house? We can call in the crime scene to the tower, right? Or should we just contact the police once we get back?" Flynn asked.

"Yes, I've got the latitude and longitude," Derek confirmed, grateful that the discussion had veered away from the army and into new territory. "I'll call these in to the tower right now. I'm sure they'll want to come check out this mess ASAP."

Suddenly, before he even had a chance to reach for his radio, he saw movement out of the corner of his eye. Two men, both dressed in dark, heavy winter coats, had come out of the house and were standing in the snow. They were also both holding high-powered rifles, and before he could react, they started shouting and pointing their weapons at the helicopter.

The first bullet ripped into the window by Flynn's head, causing a crack in the glass that looked like a lightning strike. More bullets followed closely behind the first.

"Look out!" Kevin yelled, panic tingeing his voice.

"Get down," Flynn shouted as she motioned for Kevin to move lower on his seat. Apparently, she still couldn't see the shooters from her angle, and she huddled against the door while also trying to get a better look at what was happening. Another loud bang cracked through the air, and the aircraft dipped precariously.

A buzzer sounded, and a couple of lights flashed from the dashboard. Derek responded immediately by turning the aircraft away from the shooters and revving the engine to escape the onslaught, but he wasn't quite fast enough.

Another bullet ripped into the back of the helicopter, and a plume of smoke began pouring from the engine, floating ominously toward the sun. Derek immediately corrected the flight trajectory, but there was only so much he could do as the aircraft limped away from the scene. At this point, he instinctively knew there was no way they were going to make it back to the flight line. All he wanted to do was get the helicopter as far away from the shooters as possible and find a safe place to land.

The gunmen fired several other shots, but Derek flew in an erratic pattern that he'd learned from the firefights he'd flown in the sandbox. No other bullets hit the helicopter, but he was losing altitude fast and trying to compensate as best he could as he studied the terrain. Smoke continued to billow from behind the helicopter and filled the air. If nothing else, he hoped it helped camouflage their exact location—at least a little—from the shooters.

"We've been hit," he said over and over again into his microphone as he tried to transmit their location and the call numbers from his helicopter to the tower. Static was his only response, and he wasn't even sure the tower was receiving his messages. Apparently, the radio had been damaged, or there was some other problem. A gust of wind lifted his helicopter and pushed him farther south than he wanted to go, and he quickly adjusted. He hadn't had to fly like this since his last flight in Syria, and he had to push away from his mind's eye images of the crash that had taken his friend's life. Jax Thomas had been his copilot and had been flying with him on that awful day when they'd taken fire. A bullet had caught their rear rotor and crashed the helicopter. Despite all his efforts, Derek hadn't been able to save his friend, and the crash still haunted him today. Guilt followed him around like a constant companion, robbing him of any joy that tried to trickle into his life. He didn't deserve happiness. His friend would never again be able to enjoy the good things in life, so why should he? The memory of Jax's death was like carrying a heavy stone around day in and day out. The painful recollections weighed him down, so much so that many times, he felt like he was just going through the motions as he tried to get through another day. Was this crash also going to kill someone he had cared about?

Another gust of wind took them higher, and he could tell that he was fast losing control of the aircraft. His speed increased, and smoke, burning smells and heat permeated the cabin. There had to be a fire in his engine compartment, and he studied his instruments carefully, trying to verify and isolate the problem.

He flattened his lips, and his jaw tensed. According to the readings, his entire engine was on fire. The heat in the cabin was almost unbearable.

Derek kept shouting into his headset, but there was no response from the tower. He tried one last time. "Mayday, mayday. We're going down!"

TWO

Derek glanced over at Flynn. Her left hand grasped the seat beneath her, and her right grabbed the door frame for dear life. She was gripping the plastic handle so tightly her knuckles were turning white. Her curly light brown hair was pulled back from her face with a light blue headband, and her blue eyes had rounded so he could see the fear overwhelming her. She had a smattering of freckles across her cheeks, and each one stood out in contrast against the paleness of her skin—even more so now. His heart constricted as he felt beads of sweat popping out across his brow, and his jaw ached from gritting his teeth.

Derek turned and quickly moved his focus back to flying the helicopter and getting them on the ground. He couldn't lose Flynn and Kevin like he had lost Jax in the Middle East. He had to land safely. He quickly turned off his fuel, the heater, the defroster and anything else he could reach as he tried to keep the helicopter under control. They were dropping even faster, and he rapidly searched for a landing site that would be both safe and far enough away from the shooters that they would have a fighting chance to survive.

They came across a small clearing that just might

work, and Derek pulled hard on the throttle, trying to decrease speed as he lowered the collective and aimed for the spot. He was losing his hydraulics and had to exert quite a bit of force to get the controls to work, but they slowly did as he required. As his hands worked the collective and the cyclic, he used his feet to operate the antitorque pedals to control the direction the helicopter was pointing in. Gently, he increased the pressure on the left pedal to swing the nose in that direction, trying to avoid all contact with the trees and a nearby outcrop of rocks. He hoped he was at least two hundred feet away from any obstacles that might cause him to crash and kill them all, or cause even further damage to his helicopter, but with the heavily billowing smoke, it was hard to get a read on their actual distance or location. He glanced again at his landing site that was on the right side of helicopter and grimaced as he adjusted the trim once again.

The airspeed dipped to about forty knots as he began his descent. Even so, the vertical speed was still a bit too fast, and he pushed hard on the collective control, but it was nearly impossible to lower the velocity much as gravity pulled against them. Derek frowned and pushed up on the nose, then breathed a sigh of relief as the airspeed dropped to thirty knots, then twenty. That movement obscured his vision of the landing area even further, but it was necessary to keep them from slamming into the snowy ground below.

The helicopter moved forward a few more feet, and Derek reduced the collective even more. He armed the parking brake, then eased the cyclic control back to reduce momentum. Then he slowly moved the stick forward to level the altitude. He kept the rate of descent as slow as possible, adjusting the collective as he did so, and felt the helicopter touch the ground. Derek wasn't sure how deep the snow was beneath him, but after another few seconds, he made contact with the earth itself and heaved an inward sigh of relief.

He verified that his parking brake was armed and then reduced and cut all power to the helicopter. Thick gray plumes of smoke billowed around them as the rotors began to slow. He quickly unbuckled his seat belt and turned to Kevin.

"Hand me that fire extinguisher," he ordered brusquely.

Kevin was shaken, but Derek's firm voice shocked the boy into compliance.

Derek took the small canister, then met Flynn's eyes. "Both of you, please get out and get as far away from the helicopter as you can, but keep your eyes open for the shooters, and try to hold your breath as much as you can so these fumes don't make you sick." They both nodded, and he could tell by their expressions that they understood the seriousness of the situation and would follow his directions. He pushed open his door and jumped out of the helicopter, then released the catch on the engine compartment and started spraying the metal down with the white foam that came spewing out of the extinguisher. As he suspected, the smoke was suffocating, and he paused a time or two to draw his shoulder up to his mouth and inhale through the fabric of his navy flannel shirt, hoping to get even the smallest amount of clean air. His chest tightened as he struggled to breathe and handle the relief that was also coursing through him. They had made it safely to the ground, but the shooters might be only a few steps behind them. Tightness pulled against his chest.

He glanced over at Flynn, who had taken the boy over to the tree line. She still looked pale and terrified. Of all the women who had to lease his helicopter today, why did it have to be her?

Derek had loved her once, back in college, although he had given her up when he joined the army. Unfortunately, he'd realized he'd made a huge mistake the minute he got on that plane to go to basic training, but at that point, he'd already destroyed the relationship, and he'd convinced himself there was no turning back. He had been terrified of settling down and having a family, so he had escaped, and run as fast and as far away as he could. His life growing up had been no picnic—his father had been an angry and physically abusive man who had made Derek's life miserable until the older man had finally succumbed to a heart attack a couple of years ago. How could he guarantee he wouldn't be the same kind of parent? He'd never been good around children, and Flynn had wanted a family—complete with a dog and white picket fence.

He glanced at her again, and his grip tightened. He'd dated since then, telling himself that he'd finally gotten over her, but every woman he'd gone out with had always been a pale imitation of Flynn who had captured his heart all those years ago. She was the most beautiful woman he'd ever seen, with curly brown hair that begged to be toyed with and blue eyes the color of the sea after a storm.

He turned his head slightly, forcing himself to look away from Flynn and focus on their current situation.

He had no business even thinking about Flynn right now beyond trying to keep her and her nephew safe. She deserved better than a has-been military pilot who had let his best friend get killed in the Middle East. The love he'd felt for her had never truly disappeared, but he couldn't pursue Flynn now…or ever. He'd already broken her heart once, and he knew she'd never trust him again.

Though they had landed and were all in one piece, Flynn felt paralyzed with fear. She had been alive for nearly thirty years and had been in mortal danger on more than one occasion on the job. However, having someone trying to shoot her out of the sky was a new experience that scared her on an entirely new level.

Unfortunately, their troubles were just beginning. They were near the top of a mountain peak in the Colorado Rockies with a damaged helicopter that she doubted would fly again before the engine received major repairs. They had no supplies that she knew of, killers were undoubtedly going to show up at any minute, and despite her coat and lightweight gloves, the snowy cold weather chilled her to the bone.

Not to mention the fact that her eleven-year-old nephew was standing beside her, and she was responsible for his welfare. Would they survive this?

She had to do this. Regardless of her own fear, she had to be strong for Kevin. She turned slightly so she could see the boy. His face was ashen and stood out in stark relief against his dusty blond hair and dark brown eyes. "Are you okay?"

"Yeah, but I don't think I ever want to ride on a helicopter again." Kevin shivered.

"Agreed." She had grabbed her camera bag before the two of them had run over to the tree line, and as she adjusted the strap on her shoulder, she noticed for the first time that Kevin was also carrying a small bag.

"What have you got in there?" she asked.

"Just some snacks," he mumbled. "I figured we might get hungry."

She gave him a reassuring nod as she quickly took her camera strap from around her neck and removed the SD card that contained the crime-scene photos. She found a blank SD card in a side pocket of her backpack and inserted that into the body. Next, she slid the small card with the crime-scene photos into a protective plastic cover and thrust it deeply into one of her gloves. She stowed her camera back in her bag and placed it by the trunk of a large aspen tree. The backpack contained some pretty expensive equipment, but she opted to leave everything behind anyway. If she had to guess, they'd be walking until they found help, and she didn't want the heavy bag to hamper their escape. It was hard to be so practical, but she figured that since her life—and Kevin's—depended on safely navigating down the mountain, she didn't want to be hindered by the backpack or worry about the contents as they traveled. She did have a small waterproof pocket camera, which she stowed in her jacket. She couldn't imagine needing it but figured there was no harm in keeping it with her due to its slight size and weight. Hopefully, they would be able to return to the helicopter's crash site with help from local law enforcement and she could retrieve her bag again. But even if the camera didn't survive the cold or the elements, keeping the equipment safe wasn't worth her life.

They watched Derek from the tree line, which was about sixty feet away from the downed helicopter. He had finished with the fire extinguisher, and although the billowing gray smoke had lessened a bit and turned whiter in color, there was still quite a bit floating through the air. He shook his head, and Flynn could see his frustration in his expression and body language. She hoped he had insurance, but either way, this horrible event was going to put him out of business for days, if not weeks. She had no idea about his financial solvency but imagined a helicopter operation was not a cheap endeavor and retrieving the helicopter from this remote, snowy mountainside was not going to be easy. She hoped the bird was fixable, but another wave of guilt swept over her. Why hadn't she just stayed at the hospital with her sister?

As they kept an eye out, Derek grabbed a few things from the helicopter and put them in a navy backpack, then quickly headed toward them. "I'm really sorry about all this," he said quietly once he had joined them. "But don't worry. I don't have much that will help us, but I do have an emergency kit with a few vital items, and I know quite a bit about surviving in difficult situations. I promise I'm going to do everything I can to get us safely back to town."

"This is my fault, not yours," Flynn murmured. "Any chance you can fix that helicopter?"

"Not without help and some new parts. The bullets caused too much damage."

He ran his fingers through his short dark hair in a show of exasperation. "The first thing we need to do is put as much distance as we can between us and this helicopter. All this smoke is basically acting like a beacon for the shooters right now. Those guys could show up at any second. Are you ready to move?"

Flynn glanced at what Kevin was wearing and winced. He had not planned to be out trekking through the snow, and his clothes were better suited for hanging out with friends or watching a movie instead of spending any time outdoors. His jacket was thin, and although he had on a knit hat, he was wearing canvas tennis shoes and didn't have any gloves. "Yes, unless you have any warmer clothes in that helicopter for Kevin. He's not wearing much to keep him warm."

Derek shook his head. "Unfortunately, I don't, but he can take my gloves." He quickly stripped them off and handed them to the boy, who immediately put them on. "Okay, let's go." Derek motioned into the forest with his head, then started moving toward the trees, his motions quick and efficient.

Flynn and Kevin followed closely behind him despite his long stride. Her mind whirled as she watched him make his way through the snow. She glanced at Derek's sidearm that was secured at his waist, along with an extra magazine. The fact that he was armed made her feel somewhat safer, regardless of what he'd stowed in the backpack. She was a good shot herself, but she also knew Derek must have received extensive training in the military. She'd been angry when he'd chosen the service over their relationship back in college, but now she found herself thankful that he was so prepared. The trek back to civilization wouldn't be easy, but with Derek along, she acknowledged that they at least had a fighting chance. She was a Florida girl, born and raised, and only had a vague idea of what it would take to survive in the snow.

Suddenly, they heard voices closing in. Derek turned and motioned for them to follow him, and they quickly ran several yards and ducked behind a fallen log. Right before joining them, Derek grabbed a nearby fallen branch and used the dried leaves to brush the snow and hide their footprints. He dived into their hiding place just as two men emerged from the nearby trees.

"I see the helicopter," the first man said as he pointed toward the clearing. He was wearing a green puffy coat and jeans, a black knit hat, and thick leather gloves. "I told you I was going to knock it out of the sky." He laughed callously. "That metal bird is still smoking."

Flynn laid a careful hand on Kevin's back, hoping to reassure him. He was close in front her, and Derek was directly behind her, his body curled protectively around hers like a shield. She turned her head so that she could see into his eyes, and the confidence she saw there helped calm her racing heart, even as she stiffened at his touch. Despite her law enforcement training, she was scared—more for Kevin's sake than her own. She had to protect her nephew, no matter the cost. Derek said nothing, but reached for her hand and gave it a squeeze as he nodded slightly, apparently understanding her angst. He was so close, she could smell the mint on his breath and see the dark flecks in his stormy blue eyes. There was some awkwardness in his response, yet he still did his best to try to comfort her. Derek's touch made her feel safe, which surprised her, even though she'd flinched at the contact. She had been avoiding most touch for quite a while—especially by men—even if it was innocent or just a friendly gesture. Her attention went back to their pursuers, and she could hear their feet crunching in the snow as they approached.

"Yeah, yeah," the second man responded. He was wearing similar clothing but had on a blue jacket instead of green. "The helicopter is huge—at least as big as my truck. How could you miss? You're no sharpshooter. Anyone could have shot that thing out of the sky."

"I didn't just hit it," Green Jacket boasted. "I got the engine. That thing won't be flying for a while, I can tell you that."

The other man's voice sounded bored. "I couldn't care less. Let's just find the pilot and the passengers, finish them off, and get back to the house. It's freezing out here."

"Like they're gonna survive in this snow anyway," Green Jacket said with a grin.

The other man stopped only a few feet from where the trio was hiding. Flynn could just make out their shapes from her position on the ground. They weren't big men, but with the guns in their hands, they seemed larger and more threatening. She prayed silently and squeezed Kevin's shoulder in reassurance.

"Look, you idiot. They saw the meth lab. They saw the bodies in the field. They're witnesses, and we can't go back and get out of this snow until they're all dead. No loose ends, got it?"

"Yeah, okay. But it sure is cold out here. I'm telling you, they won't survive, even if we never find them."

"Just shut up and do your job." Blue Jacket shrugged and glanced around the area. "The others will be here soon. Let's get this over with."

Flynn tensed at the man's words, but Derek gave her shoulders a squeeze of reassurance. She knew, despite their past and difficult breakup, that he would do everything he could to keep her safe. The protectiveness was clearly visible in his eyes.

After a few minutes, the two men continued away from the small group, unaware that the people they were hunting for were huddling in the snow and hidden by the brush only a few feet away. Flynn glanced over at Derek, but he silently shook his head, letting her know it wasn't time to move just yet. She turned her head so she could see their adversaries. The man in the green jacket was a wild card and an easy target, but the blue-jacketed man was a more serious opponent, and both of them carried .30-06 Springfield rifles with scopes—very deadly weapons with quite a range.

A few minutes later, the men moved farther away, and Derek finally raised up slightly and sneaked a peek over the log. "Back up and crawl after me. Stay low and close," he whispered. He released Flynn's hand and began to crawl away from the scene, and Flynn and Kevin followed, trying to keep as low as possible. They hid behind brush and trees until they were a good forty feet from where they'd been hiding by the logs. Finally, a few minutes later, Derek stood and reached out his hand, helping both of them to their feet one at a time.

"Stay close, and stay quiet," Derek ordered in a whisper.

Flynn and Kevin nodded and followed Derek wordlessly into the forest, not even stopping to brush the snow from their clothes. Derek set a brutal pace, but the two stayed close, struggling some with the depth of the snow at times, but both doing their best to keep up.

They continued on for at least forty-five minutes, none of them saying a word as they trudged through the trees and the snow. The boy's teeth had started chattering, and Flynn knew her own face was pink from exertion and the cold. Thankfully, she had donned leather hiking boots for the trip on a lark, but Kevin's canvas sneakers were more suitable for a grassy field in summer than this heavy snow. They were soaking wet and his feet had to be freezing. Still, to his credit, he said nothing, although he did cup his gloved hands together and blow on them from time to time, then worked his fingers to keep the blood flowing.

They came upon another clearing, and Derek motioned for them to stop. "Stay at the tree line and out of sight. I see something up ahead," he said quietly.

Flynn nodded, then watched him head to the eastern side of the field where a bit of blue was sticking up. A sickening feeling swept over her as she watched Derek approach the mound that was partially covered by snow. Kevin had sunk down to sit on a fallen tree trunk, and she moved to block his field of vision as she watched Derek move cautiously, then circle the darkened snow.

Across the distance, their eyes met, and Derek shook his head and rubbed his eyes. A sickening feeling twisted in her stomach.

Derek had found yet another dead body.

THREE

Derek stepped carefully around the red that had splattered in the snow surrounding another gunshot victim. This body was a short young man, probably in his early twenties, with scruffy brown hair tucked loosely under a green knit cap. He was lying on his stomach and had been shot in the back as he'd run away from whoever had been pursuing him. Slowly Derek rolled him over, searching for any signs of life. His lips were blue, and his skin was pallid and mottled with sores, and he had damaged teeth, as if he used methamphetamine. Derek felt sure the man was dead, but reached for his neck anyway, feeling for a pulse.

There was no heartbeat. He readjusted his fingers, just in case, then pulled back. The young man was definitely lifeless, but his dark brown eyes still held a look of terror. Apprehension twisted in Derek's gut. He'd hoped to never see death again—especially so up close. He tried to push his anxiety aside and began searching the victim's body. He found a Smith & Wesson M&P Shield 9mm pistol in the man's waistband and pulled the pistol out and checked the magazine. The mag was full—eight bullets with an additional bullet in the chamber. Nine shots. Derek still had his own pistol with an extra mag, but with armed men chasing them, it would be good to arm Flynn as well.

She'd always been a tough, independent lady, and it didn't surprise him in the least that she had already become a detective despite her young age. As far as he knew, it usually took someone several years longer to reach that level in law enforcement, but Flynn was smart and driven—two great qualities that undoubtedly helped pave the way for her to reach her career goals.

Derek pocketed the new pistol. Flynn's firearm training would definitely come in handy if they met up with their pursuers before they made it back to town, and at this point, they needed all the help they could get to survive this challenge.

He glanced over at Flynn and Kevin, verifying that they were still safe, then searched the man's pockets, just in case he had an extra mag secreted somewhere on his body. There wasn't one, but he did find the man's wallet that contained a few bucks and an I.D. The victim's Colorado driver's license matched the face of the corpse. It was definitely the same man, despite the fact that the body now had the definite telltale signs of a meth user—he was thinner and had aged considerably since the photo was taken. Derek pocketed the license and replaced the wallet, hoping he would have the chance to give the card to law enforcement once they arrived safely back home. He hoped the authorities wouldn't have trouble finding the body, but if his adversaries tried to cover up their crimes, they would probably dispose of the bodies as soon as possible, and the license and Derek's eyewitness testimony could be all that proved the man was indeed dead. Somewhere, the victim might have a family who needed to know that this young man was never coming home.

He studied the man's body once again and made a swift decision. He'd already messed up the crime scene to verify the man was truly dead, and Kevin was freezing and was just a little bit smaller than the victim. He quickly pulled off the man's jacket, boots and gloves and headed back over to where Flynn and Kevin were still waiting for him at the tree line. He glanced at their clothing and noted Flynn's jeans, burgundy flannel shirt and T-shirt underneath. She also wore a decent winter coat and hiking boots, but the boy's clothing was completely inadequate.

"See if these fit," Derek said as he held the clothing out to Kevin.

Kevin raised his eyebrows, a look of disdain and horror on his face. "You're kidding, right? There's blood on those."

"Yeah, but they will keep you from freezing."

"I'm not wearing those, and you can't make me," Kevin said with a slight tremble in his voice. He was probably trying to sound defiant, but that goal was hard to accomplish with his teeth chattering because of the cold, and the sound he emitted was more of a whine.

Derek was ex-military—an officer. He didn't have time for obstinate kids, especially those giving an attitude when all their lives were at stake. He glanced over at Flynn and was about to blister the boy's ears when Flynn subtly shook her head. Her concerned expression gave him pause and held him back.

"Kevin, you don't have a choice," she said softly, her

tone filled with understanding but still laced with firmness. "I know it's tough, but your feet and hands will freeze without boots and gloves, and Derek needs his gloves back to protect his own hands. We don't know how long we're going to be up here on this mountain in this snow. It could take us days to walk down, and the temperature is already dropping pretty fast."

"When you get frostbite, you'll lose your fingers and toes. Without that coat, you might also lose your life," Derek added, his voice leaving no room for argument, a scowl on his face.

Kevin curled his lip. "There's blood on the coat, and a hole where the bullet went through the back."

"Yes," Derek agreed. "But there's only a little blood, and like I said, they will keep you from freezing to death."

Kevin took a step back, still not taking the items from Derek's outstretched hands. "I can't wear this stuff, Aunt Flynn," he whined, his voice sounding strangled. "It's gross."

"It's not up for debate. Put the clothes on. Now." Mindful of Flynn's concern, and the fact that her nephew's mom was still fighting for her life back in the hospital, Derek kept his voice firm but nonthreatening. For a moment, Derek thought the boy was still going to refuse. There was even defiance in the youth's eyes that burned with resentment, but finally he took the boots first and tried them on. They were actually a decent fit and only slightly too big, as were the gloves. The boy handed Derek's gloves back, and Derek quickly put them on.

"So what do I do with my old shoes?" the boy asked.

"Carry them or leave them. That's up to you," Derek replied. "Now try the coat."

Kevin balked, and even put his fingers through the bullet holes in the back panel, but wisely kept his mouth shut and finally acquiesced. The jacket was a bit large on him but still offered him more warmth that his own thin jacket could provide, and Derek knew that despite the blood, unless they were rescued pretty soon, the coat and other items could very well save the boy's life.

"All right. Let's keep going…" His words were cut off by the sound of a bullet whizzing by his ear and ricocheting off a nearby tree branch. "Get down!" he whispered fiercely, grabbing Flynn's hand and pulling her into a crouch behind a larger tree trunk. Bits of wood spit into the air and littered the snow right in front of them as another round hit the sapling close to the first.

"We know you're back there!" a male voice shouted from a distance. "We won't hurt you if you come out with your hands up now!"

Derek held his finger to his lips and shook his head. If they came out, they were as good as dead. It was painfully obvious that the drug dealers would do whatever was necessary to get rid of any witnesses to their criminal enterprise. He had a downed helicopter to prove it. They needed to get out of there—and fast.

Flynn's heart was beating so hard, she was sure the sound was going to get them killed. The pounding in her chest and the roaring in her ears were so loud she just knew they had to be audible to those around her. She'd been in tight spots before, but never with her nephew in tow and under her care. Her vision swam and the trees started spinning right before her eyes. How had this afternoon turned into a disaster so quickly? She had wanted to give Kevin a break from the hospital walls and distract him from his mother's situation.

Putting his life in danger had not been part of her plan.

She glanced at Derek, who was crouching next to her and taking stock of the situation. She could almost see his brain working, considering options, figuring out a plan of escape. She might not recognize this professional yet detached soldier as her boyfriend from her college days, but she couldn't have picked a better person to be stranded in the woods with. Despite the years that had passed, and her general distrust of men in relationships, she knew instinctively that the two of them would make a good team as they fought this adversary together. He moved slightly and handed her a pistol, and she gave him a smile, flipped the safety off and checked the magazine. Nine shots.

Things were looking up.

She met Derek's eyes, and he motioned for her and Kevin to follow him, crouching down and moving silently and quickly through the forest, away from the men with the rifles. There was no use having a showdown if it wasn't necessary, and her primary goal was getting Kevin to safety. They moved from tree to tree, using them as shields and camouflage as they tried to put as much distance as possible between them and the criminals pursuing them.

Dear God, please help us. The prayer was short but heartfelt. She had been moving away from God during the last few years, but she knew intuitively that her reticence was a mistake. She needed to draw closer to God, not pull away. She needed God in her life more than ever, especially now with a pair of killers bearing down on them.

They had gotten about thirty feet away from their original location when one of the shooters opened fire again. Bits of bark rained down on them as they raced from tree to tree, trying to stay safe and ahead of the shooters' onslaught.

Flynn staggered over a tree limb and hit the ground hard, but when a bullet hit a tree in front of her, she realized that the fall had actually saved her life. If she'd been vertical, the bullet would have no doubt caught her in the chest. She pulled herself to her feet, ignoring the throbbing pain that had begun in her left knee when she'd landed, and kept running. Derek was leading the way, and Kevin was between them, and that was just the way she wanted it. Derek would undoubtedly know the best way to go, and she needed to have Kevin in front of her and in her line of sight so she knew he was safe and keeping up with them.

Snowdrifts slowed them down—in some areas the snow was over a foot thick, and she struggled to pull her feet up and take the next step. The conditions made it hard to outrun the reach of the high-powered rifles the shooters were using. The only consolation was that the difficult environment was also slowing down their pursuers. The shots continued, and each bullet sent another jolt of fear thorough her as she ran. She couldn't lose Kevin, especially not when her sister was fighting for her life in the hospital. She had to keep him safe. The thought of losing both of them terrified her as the adrenaline pumped through her veins.

Suddenly, she saw Derek pull himself up short and

stop. As she approached, she could see that he'd reached a ledge and there was apparently a drop in front of him. He grabbed Kevin and quickly pulled him behind a stand of bushes, and she joined them a few seconds later and looked down past their feet into the gorge that loomed below.

They were stuck. The area below was at least forty feet down—maybe even more. She had never been good at estimating distances, but the sight scared her. Rock climbing had never been her thing, but at least she was in fairly good shape—she could probably make it down without too much trouble. But what about Kevin? She took another look. In certain places, the snow had piled up against the bank of the ledge at the bottom of the gorge, but it was impossible to know how deep the slush was or what was beneath it. The three crouched down, trying to make themselves as small as possible as they figured out their next move. They couldn't go back. But how could they get down the ledge safely?

"Now what?" Flynn asked breathlessly, her eyes meeting Derek's.

"We climb down the rocks. There is no other option. The shooters have us pinned down." Derek looked directly at Kevin. "Can you handle this?"

The boy shrugged, but Flynn could tell he was putting on an act as he tried to infuse toughness into his voice. "Do I have a choice?"

"I don't see one," Derek mumbled, apparently more to himself than in response. His expression was filled with frustration. It was obvious that he shared Flynn's concerns about getting Kevin to the bottom. "Kevin, come behind me, so if you have any trouble, I can try to help you. There are some deep snowdrifts down there, so if either of you start to slip, try to slide toward one that can help cushion your fall." He swung his legs over the edge. "Okay. Let's do this. Grab the branches or other hand-holds when you can, and follow me down."

More bullets sounded around them, and stealth was immediately forgotten as they scurried over the ledge and started their descent. Flynn didn't have time to think about the distance between her or the ground—or the lack of handholds available on the snowy surface of the vertical rock wall. She just started climbing down, her mind focused on escape and making sure Kevin and Derek were nearby and safely descending.

Suddenly, her left hand slipped, and she searched frantically for a new handhold. Her glove grappled around the area, looking for anything that would help support her weight, but she found only dirt and bits of rock that dislodged and fell as she tried to grasp something new for support. Her right hand was holding a root that was protruding out a few inches, but even as she tried to find a new handhold for her left, she felt her right hand slipping down the root. The narrow stem was simply too small to support her, and she realized fleetingly that she was only seconds away from plummeting to the ground. Her body swayed, then started slowly sliding as the root slipped through her fingers and gravity pulled her down the face of the wall. She wanted to scream, but she swallowed the sound, unwilling to give her attackers any more clues about their whereabouts. Instead, she gritted her teeth as fear coursed through her veins, her jaw tight as she slid awkwardly down the rocky surface, unsure if she would survive the next few minutes.

FOUR

Flynn landed in a deep pile of snow and lay still for a moment, surprise mixed with relief making her breath shallow and fast. She was still alive. A quick but near-silent prayer of thanksgiving issued from her lips as she started to move, carefully at first, making sure there weren't any rocks or other solid hazards buried around her. She rolled to the right, the snow crunching beneath her weight as she struggled to her knees. A few seconds later, both Kevin and Derek were by her side, worry painted across both of their features.

"Are you okay?" Kevin asked, his eyes wide as Derek reached over and helped her to her feet. "I got so scared when I saw you fall! I thought you were dead!" He kept his voice low, even though it was filled with anxiety.

"I'm okay." She shook herself, trying to regain her bearings. "That was quite a ride." She whispered, knowing the gunmen were still close by and hunting them. She looked down at her jeans, where there was a small tear, and smiled to herself. God had truly been watching out for her. She could barely believe that after being chased through the woods and falling down the rocky ledge, she was relatively unscathed and had only a sore knee and a small rip in her pants to show for it. She said another silent prayer of thanks, then took a deep breath. "Let's get out of here before those killers follow us down."

Derek nodded. "Good plan."

She glanced at his expression and saw what she thought was genuine concern and something more filling his eyes. Before she could think that much about his countenance, he had already turned and started leading them away from the bottom of the rocky wall. Back in college, she could read him like a book. Now? She had no idea what he was thinking.

Suddenly, a bullet ricocheted off a nearby rock, and Flynn flinched involuntarily as she heard noises from above. Adrenaline coursed through her chest as she quickly motioned to her nephew to move toward the trees. He followed her directions, and she trailed closely behind him, searching the area above them for any sign of their attackers as she did so. She couldn't see them, but she could hear them shouting, and she figured they were just firing randomly, hoping to hit a target. She considered pulling her pistol and firing back but knew instinctively that she had little chance of hitting a target from this distance and angle, even if she did manage to get one of the criminals in her sights. Her pistol didn't have the range or accuracy of the rifles that the shooters were using. And with limited ammunition, there was no use wasting it when she might very well need it later on. Keeping her weapon secure, Flynn followed Kevin and moved to cover.

"They're headed west!" a man yelled, and his voice echoed off the canyon walls as another bullet followed closely behind the first.

Maybe they weren't shooting randomly after all. Flynn grabbed Kevin's hand and followed closely behind Derek, who had taken refuge behind an outcrop of rock as he waited for them to catch up. He motioned for them to follow him and headed deeper into the aspen forest at a fast clip. They used the tree trunks and brush as cover the best they could, and thankfully, the snow wasn't as deep here, so they were able to make good time and put quite a bit of distance in between themselves and the attackers. Eventually, the shooters stopped firing, and they could no longer hear their voices. Finally, they all paused and caught their breath, taking in their new surroundings while still being mindful of the threat behind them.

"Do you think they're still following us?" she asked cautiously.

"Yes, but I don't think they're willing to chance going down that cliff. They're going to have to find another way around to get down to this level. By the time they do, I'm hoping we'll be long gone." He avoided her eyes and turned. "Let's keep moving. The more distance we can put between us and them, the better."

They kept moving down the side of the mountain, hiking as quickly as they could manage for what seemed like hours. They said very little and stayed near the trees whenever possible. Thankfully, they didn't see their pursuers following them and heard nothing more. Even so, they knew the shooters had to be following them, closing in, dogging their heels.

For the most part, Flynn followed Derek's lead, but later that afternoon, when Kevin's stamina started to wane and his steps slowed, she waved to Derek and motioned out of Kevin's sight that they needed to talk. They had stopped a couple of times already to rest, but at this point, Flynn was convinced that Kevin was completely spent. The boy was only eleven, after all, and though he was of average height and build for a boy his age, he wasn't used to the strenuous activity of hiking through snow for hours at a time. He plopped himself down on a fallen log and his shoulders slumped. The stress from exertion showed in his haggard expression and exhausted body language. Flynn was tired herself, and her knee was throbbing. She couldn't imagine how Kevin was still managing to stay on his feet.

"We need to stop," Flynn murmured for Derek's ears alone, still very much aware of the necessity of keeping her voice low, just in case their enemies were in earshot. She motioned with her head, not wanting her nephew to hear her concerns, either. "Kevin can't go any farther." She swallowed and absently rubbed her leg above her injured knee. "I feel like we've been going in circles, but I'm sure you have a reason. Do you have plans for the night?"

"I do," he said softly as he raised an eyebrow. "And yes, we have been backtracking for about the last hour. When we slid down that cliff, I noticed a rock formation to the southwest that might offer us some refuge from the elements. We passed the area once, but now we're going back. I'm hoping the guys with the guns will think we continued on down the mountain. Most people don't turn around and look behind them when they're searching for someone."

"Smart move," she said with a tired smile. "Are we close?"

Derek nodded. "Another fifteen minutes or so ought to do it, but we'll still need to keep our voices down. I heard them say something about reinforcements, and I don't know how many others might be looking for us or how spread out they are. I do think those guys are going to be combing these woods until they find us, though. Like the guy said—we're a loose end. They can't allow us to get back to town. They know we'll report what happened and what we saw."

"I'm sorry I'm not much help," she said softly. "Hiking in the outdoors has never been my thing."

"I remember," he said so softly she wasn't even sure she'd actually heard the words. For a moment he seemed lost in memories, but then he suddenly looked up, his expression clear. "Stay close. It won't be much farther." He turned away and, without another sound, started walking again.

Flynn watched him for a moment or two, not quite sure what to make of him, then made eye contact with Kevin and gave him a soft smile. His nose was red and his shoulders slouched. "We're almost done for the day. I know you're tired, but can you make it another fifteen minutes?"

"I guess," he responded, his tone weary. "I just want to get away from those guys."

"We're going to make it," she affirmed, her tone confident. "You're doing great, Kevin. Just a little bit farther and we'll stop for the night and get some rest." She motioned toward Derek's retreating figure. "He's good. Really good. You don't need to worry. He'll make sure we make it down this mountain."

"Seems like you guys are friends, or used to be," Kevin said as he slowly pulled himself up and they started to follow Derek again. He kept his voice down, but there was genuine interest in his tone. "How do you know him?"

"Derek was actually my boyfriend back in college, if you can believe it. Remember how I told you I went to school at Florida State in Tallahassee? Well, so did he. I haven't talked to him in years, though, and I was surprised to see him at the airport. I didn't even know he lived out here in Colorado. But I do know he was always good at getting out of a jam. You can trust him."

"Uh-huh," Kevin answered, apparently not convinced.

Flynn didn't respond. She wanted to reassure her nephew but didn't want to continue the conversation when danger could very well be around every corner. She gave him a gentle nudge, hoping to help him find his second wind. "We're going to make it," she said softly. "Don't give up."

Derek glanced behind him, verifying that Flynn and Kevin were only about twenty feet back. The snow was patchy here around the trees, and the walking was a bit easier than it had been when they had been more out in the open and farther east. Considering the boy's condition, he was grateful for the change, even though he knew the easier conditions wouldn't last. Most of the mountain was already covered with snow, and the forecast called for another storm to hit in the next few hours. The night would be difficult, especially if they couldn't have a fire.

His thoughts strayed back to Flynn again. His assistant had taken the reservation, and all he'd known before the flight was that a woman and boy wanted to scout out some coordinates on the mountain. He hadn't looked at the names of the passengers before arriving to perform his preflight checks. He had been floored to see Flynn standing by his helicopter on the flight line, her smile lighting up the tarmac like a warm sunny day, even though it was November, with a chill in the air.

Why was this kid with her on the flight? She'd introduced him as her nephew but hadn't given any other explanation or details about her life. He remembered that she had a sister but hadn't interacted with Erin much back in college while he'd dated Flynn and hardly recalled anything about her. Flynn had probably mentioned Kevin during college, but he just didn't remember.

Why was she even in Colorado? Questions plagued his mind as he walked.

Was Flynn married? He hadn't seen a ring, but that didn't mean much these days. Plenty of married folks in the military didn't wear jewelry to protect their hands from getting caught in machinery or weaponry. And she had mentioned that she was a new detective, which meant she must have been working in law enforcement for a few years. Earning the rank of detective was no small feat, especially at her young age. Perhaps her job had something to do with the reason why she kept her hands free of ornamentation. Or maybe she was still single...

But why did he care?

He shouldn't. *He didn't.* Flynn's marital status was none of his business. He forced his thoughts away from her. Unbidden, his mind turned to Jax, as it often did. Jax smiling as he played a practical joke on him. Jax playing the drums in their garage band as his own fingers strummed his bass guitar. Jax lying dead in the tangled heap of metal than had once been a helicopter before the bird had been shot from the sky…

Derek and Jax had joined the army together, but instead of making a career out of the service, Derek had gotten out as soon as he could after Jax was killed. Derek's guilt was crippling, even though he was exonerated of any wrongdoing by a military tribunal. Nowadays, Derek struggled to maintain a meaningful relationship with anyone. He couldn't be responsible for losing someone else close to him. Yet here he was, leading his old girlfriend and her young nephew on foot down the mountain with gunmen hot on their tails—after his helicopter was shot out of the sky again, no less! And his companion wasn't just any ex-girlfriend. It was Flynn Denning—the one he had loved with all his heart. She was the only woman who had actually made him consider settling down and having a family, even though the idea of marriage scared him right down to his toes. No one else he'd dated had come close to Flynn's feisty personality, sweet smile or caring heart. Whenever he daydreamed of a future, it was Flynn's face that appeared in his mind's eye.

But living life with Flynn by his side was a silly dream—one that could never happen.

How did he get here? Just by catching her eye before their flight, his chest had grown tight as the emotions of loss and love had nearly overwhelmed him. He'd had no choice but to bury his feelings beneath a veneer of indifference, knowing that he had lost her forever after he had signed on the dotted line and joined the army. Derek hadn't even discussed his decision with her after he'd met with the recruiter. When she'd started talking about having a family, he'd been so scared that he would turn into his father that he'd run as fast as he could in the opposite direction. Derek knew he'd handled the whole situation badly. Communication had never been one of his strong suits. But even so, his actions had never erased the love he still held for her in his heart.

Derek shook his head and gritted his teeth. Once again, he found himself trying to push the thoughts of Flynn and their past into the dark recesses of his mind. Somehow, he had to lead these two down off this mountain without getting caught by the gunmen or the elements. He didn't have time for reminiscing, daydreaming or ruminating on his prior mistakes. The past was over and done. There was no going back.

He led them to the rock formation, then motioned for them to stay covered under the trees while he explored the area. Kevin sank down to sit in the snow, and Flynn stood protectively in front of him, her sharp eyes keeping watch for any signs of danger.

Derek pushed aside some brush, careful not to break the branches and leave signs of his presence, and pulled out a small flashlight attached to his key chain. He'd revealed a narrow opening, and he ducked and twisted to squeeze between the stones. The fissure formed an awkward entrance, but after several feet, the space opened up into an oval-shaped room about ten feet wide and seven feet long. The cave had a low ceiling—he couldn't stand up all the way—but it would suit his purposes and keep them safe from the elements during the night. There didn't seem to be a back entrance beyond some small crevices in the rocks, but he did see some daylight between the stones, so at least they would have some ventilation. The only negative he could see was that if they were discovered, they would be sitting ducks. There would be no escape.

He said a silent prayer as doubts assailed him. What if he failed? What if the gun-toting drug dealers killed Flynn and her nephew on his watch? How would he ever survive that?

"Derek!"

Derek turned and pointed his flashlight at the rock opening at Flynn's urgently whispered exclamation. Kevin was on his hands and knees and entering the small space, and Flynn was right behind him in a similar position. The beam caught her eyes, which were troubled yet filled with fire.

"They're right outside…"

FIVE

Derek quickly flipped the flashlight off and pocketed it, then hurried over to help move Kevin deeper into the cave while Flynn scurried in behind him as quietly as possible. Once inside, she pulled herself into a sitting position, leaned against the rock wall, and took a moment to collect herself and gain control over the adrenaline that was pulsing through her chest. Kevin seemed to be shivering, and even though she couldn't tell if his reaction was from fear or the cold, she pulled him wordlessly into an embrace, then listened carefully. At first, all she could hear was her own breathing and the roaring in her ears, but that gradually faded away and she could hear their pursuers' voices outside the cave. Even though they were slightly muffled, they were getting louder by the second, as if the men were walking right up to their hiding place. Her muscles tensed.

"We're not going to find them way up here," the first man said. There was a definite whine in his tone.

"Yeah, well, I'm not the boss, and until the boss says stop, we keep looking, and we go to the area he tells us to search." The second man's voice was firmer. Flynn imagined he was older than the first or at least knew the boss better and the way the drug cartel worked. "Those people saw the meth lab and the three dealers the boss executed. They know too much and have to be eliminated before they ruin all our future plans. You know that. The boss made it clear that these people can't make it down the mountain alive. If they report what they saw, their statements could destroy our whole organization. I don't know about you, but I don't want to go to prison."

"It's freezing up here!" the whiner complained. "Even if we don't find them, there's no way they'll survive the night. We'll find them tomorrow when the buzzards are circling overhead. This is a waste of time."

"Maybe, but again, we can't stop looking."

"I think they've already gone farther down the mountain. They'd be crazy to still be up this high," the complainer said, his voice raised an octave. There were some shuffling noises, and Flynn could feel Kevin tense. Were the two hunters right outside the entrance having this discussion? She listened a bit more, straining to understand what was happening and the level of danger their presence posed to the three of them. The noises sounded like more than a conversation was occurring on the other side of these rocks. Flynn wouldn't be surprised if a fistfight had broken out, or at least some serious shoving. She hugged Kevin even closer. When the second man spoke again, his voice had taken on a deadly edge.

"You're probably right, but there must be twenty of us out here looking, and only three of them, and one of them is a kid. They couldn't have gotten too far away, and we've got to come across them sooner or later, understand? So shut your mouth and do what you're told. I don't want to be the one that has to tell the boss that they escaped, and I don't think you want to be that guy, either."

"Fine. Okay. I get it." The younger man had resignation in his voice, and the two must have started walking away from the cave entrance, because their voices slowly became muffled again. Shortly thereafter, Flynn couldn't even hear them anymore. She blew out a breath of relief and gave Kevin a squeeze, then realized that he had fallen asleep in her arms. She moved her left shoulder a bit to relieve the cramp but otherwise did her best not to wake him. They'd had an exhausting day, and the stress had to be affecting him, on top of all the physical exertion. His mom was in the hospital fighting for her life, and now he was out here being shot at with a cartel hot on their trail. What had she been thinking taking Kevin along to investigate her sister's notes?

She heard Derek shuffle and stretch, then he settled down a few feet away from her. If he was half as tired as she was, his muscles must be aching, too.

"What's your plan?" she asked softly.

"I thought I'd rest for a few minutes and give those guys time to clear out. Then I'll go scout the area and make sure they're gone." He shifted. "How's Kevin?"

"Dog tired. He's out for the count. He was dealing with a stressful situation anyway, and being chased by these criminals has really rocked his world. I'm amazed he's doing as well as he is."

"He's a trouper. So are you." He paused. "So, what's going on here? Why did we just stumble across some kind of drug operation?"

Flynn swallowed. "My sister, Erin, is a detective down in Frisco. She got shot a couple of days ago and is still fighting for her life in the hospital, so I flew in from Florida to be with her and help out with Kevin."

"I'm sorry," Derek said softly. "I didn't even know she lived in Colorado."

"Thanks," she replied. "She hasn't been here very long. Her husband left her and Kevin about a year ago, and she moved here, hoping to start fresh." She sniffed, trying to keep her nose from running in the cold. "Anyway, I'm trying to figure out who shot her and why, but the local folks aren't being very helpful. I found some of her notes on her desk. It looks like she was involved with a drug bust a few days before she was shot, and she was trying to get one of the dealers to flip. He mentioned this place up here on the mountain but didn't give a lot of details, and she was going to go check it out but didn't get the chance. Kevin and I were both going a little stir-crazy in the hospital, so I hoped the diversion would do us both some good. I had no idea we were going to come across a murder scene."

Flynn was tired and her emotions were on overdrive, but she still thought it was time to discuss the elephant in the room that had been plaguing her ever since she had recognized Derek this afternoon on the flight line. One of her big regrets in life was that she hadn't pushed for answers back when Derek had broken up with her, and she had always wished that she'd fought harder for their relationship. They had both said a lot of angry things, but ultimately, she had never really understood what had happened between them. All she could imagine was that she had done or said something that had driven him away. It was too late now to restore the camaraderie and love that had existed between them, but it wasn't too late to ask questions so she could finally get some closure.

"So, after graduation, I could never really figure out why you picked the army over a life with me. I know we weren't officially engaged, but I thought we were heading in that direction and planning a life together—you know, marriage, two-point-five kids, a home, a dog— the whole enchilada. Then, the next thing I know, you're ending our relationship, pretty abruptly, I might add, and heading to the Middle East to fly helicopters. Our American dream just went up in smoke with no explanation, no fanfare and not even much of a goodbye. Do you think you could enlighten me?"

Tension suddenly filled the air. It was so thick, she could feel it. Still, although she regretted the timing of her questions, she couldn't regret asking them. She'd been carrying them around for the last eight years. She held her breath, almost afraid to hear him say the words. Her feelings of self-worth had taken quite a beating during her life, but maybe if she could understand what drove men away from her, she could work on fixing the problem.

Finally, Derek spoke. "You really want to discuss this now?"

"Well, I agree the timing isn't ideal, but we may never get another chance to hash this out. If I've learned anything lately, it's that you don't always get a second chance to ask questions or tell someone what you're feeling." Her thoughts fluttered to her sister in the hospital, then returned to the situation before her. "I'd really like to know what happened. You committed to the military without even discussing it with me." She paused and swallowed.

"We said a lot of angry words after that, but I still don't understand your decision. Then you left without even really saying goodbye."

He was quiet for a long time before answering. "Why does it matter now? That was over eight years ago."

"It matters," Flynn insisted. "I was in love with you, and then from one day to the next, our relationship was over and you were going down an entirely different path—one that we hadn't even discussed. I was shocked and hurt by your actions." She chewed her bottom lip, unsure. "What did I do or say that made you run in the opposite direction? I know the problem had to be my fault. Something's wrong with me. I get it. But I don't know what I did, and I really want to understand."

Again, Derek didn't answer, and the silence seemed to swell between them. Flynn had already gone this far. She pushed ahead. "Well, whatever it was, I'd like to apologize right here and now. I never meant to push you away." She closed her eyes for a moment, glad that Derek couldn't see the tears in her eyes. She hadn't meant to cry. She hadn't even planned to discuss this. Why did Derek have to be the helicopter pilot she'd encountered on the tarmac? Still, it felt good to finally confront the pain that she still carried from their separation. It was clear she was a social disaster. But what was it about her that drove men away? She really wanted to know. Maybe, just maybe, now that so much time had passed, Derek would be able to explain what had happened. If she told him a little more, would he answer her questions? It was worth a try.

"Until about two months ago, I was seriously dating a man back in Florida named Ted. I actually thought he might be the one, you know? We were together over two years. And then I discovered he was cheating on me and had another woman on the side." She swallowed. "I guess I have some serious flaws that sent you away, just like Ted, so again, for whatever I did, I'm sorry." She blew out a breath, for a moment reliving the pain of finding out about Ted's treachery. As a result, Flynn had decided she no longer needed a man in her life and was determined to shun any and all dating relationships. It just wasn't worth the heartache that inevitably followed. The breakup with Ted had been ugly and painful, much like the breakup with Derek, albeit for different reasons. Why did the men she cared about run in the opposite direction whenever the relationships got serious? What was wrong with her?

Flynn knew she was a good detective. She had one of the best case-closure rates in her entire law enforcement organization, and her career was blossoming. So why was her personal life such a mess? Maybe, just maybe, enough time had passed that Derek could be honest with her and tell her the truth so she could uncover her problems and grow. She waited, tense, but his silence was deafening, and she wondered if her flaws were so big that he was hesitant to even talk to her about them.

Derek froze at her questions and admissions, carefully sorting through everything Flynn had just revealed. Men with guns had shot them out of the sky and were hunting them down like animals. They were running for their lives and finally had a moment to sit and regroup— and now, of all times, Flynn wanted to discuss their old relationship that had ended years ago.

Could he really blame her? He was stunned that she was shouldering the guilt for his own mistakes and actions. Derek didn't want to rip off the scabs and watch them bleed again, but he knew he hadn't been fair to her eight years ago. It had been his fault, not hers, that their relationship had ended so abruptly. He didn't like her feeling responsible, or the fact that his actions had trampled Flynn's feelings of self-worth. Besides, if they didn't talk now, when would they talk? Kevin was still asleep—he could hear the boy softly snoring. Who knew if or when they would get another private opportunity to share their thoughts?

Derek took a moment and thought back over everything that had happened back then. Flynn was right about one thing—they had really never discussed his decision to leave the relationship. And it had definitely been Derek that had left. It was no surprise that she'd been shocked and hurt by his actions. He'd known his decision would devastate her, but he'd been powerless to choose another path regardless of the pain he caused. At least he'd felt that way at the time.

He tried to look at her and make out her features so he could see what she was thinking, but it was just too dark. He could see an outline of where she was sitting with the boy but couldn't make out her expression. Maybe that was a good thing. If he could see on her face the pain that was so evident in her voice, it would probably be his undoing. Flynn had been the love of his life. He'd never had that type of relationship with anyone else and expected he never would. Flynn was one of a kind. But that level of closeness had also scared him.

Derek's own family had been dysfunctional and traumatizing, and as soon as they had started talking about marriage, he had run as fast as he could in the other direction. He was terrified that he would turn into his father the moment he said, "I do," and that would have been unthinkable. His father had been a monster, and growing up, he'd seen his mother slowly become a lonely, miserable shell of a woman. He'd learned from watching his parents' relationship that it was better to keep everyone at arm's length and avoid marriage completely. The decision resulted in a lonely existence, but that was the only way to keep from getting hurt. Even friendships caused problems. Look what his bond with Jax had cost—if he and Jax hadn't joined up together, Jax would probably still be alive.

His thoughts returned to Flynn and their time together back in Tallahassee at Florida State University. They had been so in love back then. How could he explain his fear of commitment that had basically immobilized him—and his constant dread that he would turn out to be a colossal failure as a husband and father?

He couldn't. He wouldn't. But he could help her relieve some of her own angst if she was blaming herself for their breakup. The truth was small consolation after eight years but hopefully enough to pour some salve on her wounded spirit.

"There's no need for you to apologize, Flynn. The fault was entirely mine. You didn't say or do anything that pushed me away. I just decided that I wanted something different. Marriage wasn't the right choice for me. I wasn't ready to settle down and have a family with you—or anyone else—and I guess I didn't realize it until it was too late."

Okay, that was part of the truth. He fisted his hands. He owed her the whole story. "My dad was a horrible nightmare, Flynn, and my mother wasn't much better. There's a reason why I never introduced you to them. I didn't have a great upbringing, and the idea of starting a family terrified me. I just wasn't ready. I didn't want to turn into my father."

She let those words hang for a minute or two before responding. "I always wondered why you never talked about your parents much. Even at holidays, you seemed to avoid the subject, and I didn't want to push," she said softly.

He sighed. "I had enough to eat, and they met my physical needs. I should be thankful for that. Plenty of people have it worse. But there was no love in the house, and my dad was a bully who used his fists to make sure he got his way. My mom was never strong enough to stand up to him, and she ended up drinking more often than not—probably just to escape him and the realities of her life."

He ran his tongue over his teeth, then pushed on. "I've always been embarrassed about my family, and when you started talking about starting one of our own, well, I admit, I didn't handle it well. I wasn't honest with you about my feelings and never even gave you an explanation or a chance to tell me what you were thinking. I'm sorry about that. I was truly in love with you, Flynn. I just couldn't be a husband or a father, and when I realized we were actually getting serious about tying the knot, I ran. I got scared that I would turn out to be just like my own father. I hope you can forgive me."

He really wished he could see her better. He could

hear her breathing, but she was very still and probably digesting everything he'd just said. He silently willed her to speak—to say anything to ease his conscience. He silently hoped she would also offer the forgiveness that he had been craving without even realizing it.

"I forgave you long ago." Her voice was still soft and now filled with compassion that he didn't deserve. He wondered if she would continue the discussion, and he almost wanted her to so she would answer his own questions. Was she happy? Did she miss him as much as he missed her? Yet he heard a level of resignation in her voice, as if she still wasn't completely satisfied with his answer but wasn't prepared to make herself even more vulnerable in front of him. He didn't deserve more.

He silently wondered about this man named Ted who had cheated on her. Was the man a complete idiot? Yet how could he cast stones? He certainly had been so wrapped up in his own fears and failings that he'd let this beautiful woman slip through his fingers, and he'd regretted his decision ever since.

A moment passed, then another. Flynn must have decided to let the discussion go, because she changed the subject. "So, tell me about you. What's been going on in your life for the last eight years? How'd you end up in Frisco, Colorado? I had no idea you were the King behind King Helicopter Tours. I thought you were still in the army. In fact, I thought you'd make a career out of the military."

He shrugged, even though he knew she couldn't see him very well. "I was going to, but then I was in a horrible helicopter crash, and Jax Thomas died. Did you hear about that?"

"I heard he had died, but didn't know the circumstances. The college sends out this alumni magazine twice a year, and somebody did a story about him when it happened, but they didn't give the details about his death." She paused a moment. "What happened?"

"Jax died when the helicopter I was flying got shot down during a mission in Iraq. He was my copilot."

"Oh, Derek. I'm so sorry."

Derek didn't comment. He pushed on. "Anyway, after that, I just didn't want to stay in the military any longer. I finished my time and then came out here for a fresh start—kind of like Erin, I guess. A guy I met at the local airport was selling his helicopter touring business, and the opportunity seemed like a smart investment. Next thing I know, King Helicopter Tours was up and running, and I started flying tourists around the mountains."

Flynn was quiet again, probably still processing everything he had just revealed. Jax had been in their college friend group. He and Flynn hadn't been buddies, but she had known him and spent time with him during their outings. Several times, they had all gone out to dinners, movies, hiking and even a couple of beach trips.

Once again, he found himself holding his breath, waiting to find out what she was thinking.

Would she blame him for Jax's death the way he blamed himself?

SIX

"That must have been terrible," Flynn said softly. "I had no idea. When they shot down your helicopter today, that must have brought all those memories back, and here I am opening up even more old wounds. This whole day must just be a living nightmare for you. I should have just stayed quiet. I'm so sorry."

Derek was stunned at her words. How could she not judge him? *Hate* him? And again, why was she the one apologizing? To be forgiven so easily was beyond his understanding. His voice rose as he spoke, and he instantly dropped the volume, but couldn't help the intensity. "Didn't you hear me? I just told you I killed Jax. He's dead because of me."

"I heard you. But I'm also sure that's not true."

"What?" Now he couldn't keep the incredulousness from his tone. "How can you say that?"

"Because I know you, Derek. You're not perfect. None of us are. But you cared about Jax, and there is no way you would have ever hurt him intentionally or let him get hurt if you were able to stop it from happening. You're just not capable of that type of behavior. I know that for a fact. I don't need to see an incident report or read about the details of the crash to know that. But I am sorry that he's gone, and sorry for your loss. He was a good man, too—decent and caring. I'm sure his death left a large hole in your life. I know you were close friends." She sighed. "Our country has lost way too many good soldiers and first responders, especially over the last few years. But we have to keep fighting against the drugs and other problems sweeping over the world to keep the people we love safe. We can't give up."

Derek leaned back, surprise sweeping over him from head to toe. Flynn was a cop. She probably saw a lot of the same types of ugliness on the streets that he'd seen during the war, but she seemed to think that hope still existed. Flynn continued to see the good in people. A lightness he didn't expect started to slowly seep into his chest, as if part of the burden he had been carrying had suddenly been lifted.

He pulled himself to his feet, unable to sit still any longer as the thoughts swirled within him. He needed time alone to think about everything they'd just discussed. She was right about one thing—being shot out of the sky had brought back all sorts of memories that he'd hoped he had buried forever. "I'm going out to do some surveillance. Are you okay staying here with the boy?"

"We're good, unless you need help. I can wake him up if you want me to, so I can help you…"

"No, it's better if you stay with him. I don't want him to wake up and be scared." He really did need some time alone to chew on her words and soak them in, and scouting the area to make sure the perpetrators were really gone was vital to their survival. The killers had been right about one thing—it was going to get cold tonight, and they needed to make the best of the few supplies they had with them.

Derek quietly left the cave, making sure his sidearm was easily accessible in his coat pocket. He glanced at the sky. Thankfully, it was already dusk, and the sun was slowly sinking behind the mountain. He brushed away his boot prints from the entrance to the cave, then started walking away as carefully and quietly as possible, his mind lost in memories. He glanced up again, suddenly pulling his thoughts back to the here and now and trying to remember if the moon had been full recently. He said a short prayer of thanks that the moon was new and wouldn't be shining during the evening hours. A fire to keep warm would make this night safer, but telltale smoke was out of the question. If the moon came out, there was no way they could risk one.

He paused for a moment and listened to the sounds around him. The wind whispered through the trees, and he could hear dry branches scratching against each other. Occasionally a puff of snow would fall from a tree branch and a few birds could be heard in the distance.

But what interested him was the sound of voices, not far off to his left. He froze, making sure the trees were camouflaging him as best as he could hope, and perked up his ears, hoping for any news that he could use to protect Flynn and Kevin and see them all safely down the mountain.

"Cary won't let them live. You know that."

"Of course I know that. But we have to find them first and see what they know and who they've told. I knew shooting that woman cop was going to be a problem.

Once we kill these three, the police will be all over this mountain."

Cary? Could they be talking about Adam Cary? The name was unusual, and one that Derek hadn't heard in a while. Adam Cary was the man who had sold him his helicopter tourist company that he had renamed King Helicopter Tours. Cary was also the owner of Bear Creek Vacation Rentals, or at least he had been. Derek thought the man had sold everything and moved back to Denver, but maybe he was wrong. Derek advertised his services with some of the local vacation companies, but Bear Creek wasn't one of them. There were dozens of different vacation rental companies, and Bear Creek, like the others, owned several homes throughout the Breckenridge and Frisco areas. They made a killing every time the slopes were open as skiers flocked in to enjoy the mountains. Bear Creek properties were some of the nicest—and the most expensive and exclusive. Skiers from all over the world booked into the local hotels and Airbnbs, but Derek's customers were mostly upper middle class—not the superrich that Bear Creek catered to. Derek and Cary had never really been friends or run in the same circles, but Frisco was a small town, and wealthy men like Cary got noticed.

And was Erin the "woman cop" they were referring to?

The men moved farther away from Derek, and he could no longer hear their voices clearly. He considered following them but decided against it. Job number one right now was keeping Flynn and Kevin safe. If they were talking about Adam Cary, then they had a very powerful adversary. Cary was a formidable and decisive man with abundant resources. He never did anything halfway, and if he was the one chasing them, then the mountain would be crawling with Cary's minions until they were discovered. They would have to get to safety first and then worry about stopping Cary's criminal activities. Surviving this trip, or even the night, now seemed even more improbable.

Flynn awoke with a start, Kevin's weight still heavy in her arms. How long had she been asleep? She glanced around, but all she saw was darkness. Kevin moaned and moved slightly in her arms.

"Mama?"

"No, it's Aunt Flynn."

Kevin sat up some but didn't pull away. "Where are we?"

"Still in the cave."

"Where's Mr. King?"

"He went out to do surveillance and make sure we were safe. He should be back soon." She kept her voice soft.

"I'm cold."

"I know. Me, too. Hopefully, once he gets back, we can figure out our next move. I'm hoping that involves a fire, but we'll see."

"What if the bad guys got him? What then?"

Flynn squeezed her arms around the young boy. "We just have to pray that he's safe."

Kevin made a disgusted sound with his mouth. "I don't believe in God. Praying won't work."

Flynn was surprised by this piece of news. "Why do you say that?"

Kevin leaned back against her. "I used to pray that God would bring my daddy back, but he didn't. And now my mom is hurt and might die. Then I'll be all alone. If God was real, none of that bad stuff would have happened."

Flynn had to think about how to respond to all that, and on a level an eleven-year-old would understand. He'd hit on some of the critical issues that all Christians seemed to wrestle with at some time during their walk with God—why do bad things happen to good people?

"Kevin, I am sure there is a God. I have no doubt. But sometimes we don't get what we want when we pray. The first thing you need to know is that God created all of us with free will. Do you know what that means?"

Kevin shook his head, and Flynn continued. "Well, it means we have to make our own choices. God didn't want a bunch of robots walking around on the earth. He wanted to have a relationship with each of us and to give us each the opportunity to choose whether or not we wanted to have a relationship with Him. He gave your dad the same choices." She squeezed him even tighter in a bear hug. "I know your dad left you and your mom a year ago, but that was his choice, too. He made a mistake, but sometimes we all make mistakes. See, we all get to choose how we live our lives, but we also have to deal with the consequences of our actions. And sometimes the choices we make hurt other people."

"He left because of me!"

Flynn shook her head. "That's not true, Kevin. Your mom and I talked about the situation a lot when it happened. He left for a lot of grown-up reasons that you might not understand right now, and I know he hurt you when he moved away, but it wasn't your fault. I promise you that."

Kevin was silent a long time while he digested this information. She knew her sister had talked about all this with Kevin before, but sometimes it helped to hear it again from someone else who wasn't so directly involved. Erin had shared that Kevin was swamped with self-doubt and had been exhibiting a host of behavior problems lately, especially when Erin had tried dating again. Hopefully, her words could give him a bit of reassurance.

"Do you think my mom is going to be okay?" Kevin asked, breaking into her thoughts.

"I don't know. I sure hope so. I've been praying for her ever since I heard what happened. I know it's hard not to worry about her. That's why I brought you up on this trip today. I was hoping the flight would be something fun to do to keep our minds off her medical condition." She swallowed. "I'm sorry this day turned out the way it did."

"You didn't know they would shoot at us," Kevin allowed. He reached over and patted her arm, trying in his own way to give her a bit of comfort. His actions were sweet, and she acknowledged them with a rueful smile.

"No, I sure didn't. But I want you to know that no matter what happens, you're not going to be alone. I want my sister to get better, but if she doesn't, I'll take care of you. You won't be by yourself. Okay?" Flynn felt the little boy relax against her.

"Okay," Kevin whispered.

"But I also want you to know that God is real and I'm praying for your mom every day."

"Do I have to pray, too?"

"That's your choice. But I do know that God wants to

get to know you better, and the best way for that to happen is for you to pray and read about Him in the Bible."

"Is that what you do?"

"Yep, but I have to admit, I haven't been going to church or reading the Bible as much as I should have been."

"Well, why is it important to go to church?"

"Church is where you learn even more about God," Flynn replied. "And it's like a big family. When you're with people who believe the same way you do, it makes your own faith stronger, and you get to learn together and grow at the same time." She sighed. "I need to reconnect with God myself. I let the busyness of my life get in the way, and I haven't been going to church or praying like I should have been. But ever since I got that call and came to Colorado, I've been praying a lot. This whole thing has reminded me that God and my relationship with Him need to come first in my life."

Kevin took a moment to let that sink in. Finally he spoke up. "Can we pray together?"

His voice was fragile, as if he was afraid she would refuse him, and she squeezed him again. "Of course." She said a prayer in a soft voice, asking God to keep them all safe, and to be with Erin and help the doctors know how to help her. Then she prayed for Kevin, that he would feel God's presence and that God would draw him close.

Just as she finished, she heard a noise outside. "Quiet," she whispered. "Someone's here."

SEVEN

"Flynn?"

Flynn breathed out a sigh of relief when she recognized Derek's voice. "We're here," she whispered, keeping her voice low in case any perps were still around. "Are you okay?"

"Yeah," he responded. She heard some scraping noises and moved Kevin closer to the cave wall, putting his hand out toward the rocks until he could touch the roughness to know where he was in the darkness. A dim light flickered near the entrance, and she recognized the small flashlight Derek had been using earlier. "Can you grab this wood?"

She pulled through the wood and pieces of dried leaves and bark that Derek had brought, then reached into the path and grabbed the larger logs that Derek was trying to get to her. A few minutes later, Derek pulled himself in behind the last of the wood.

"I love the idea of a fire, but is it safe?" Flynn asked.

Derek put the flashlight on the ground, then rubbed his hands together and blew into them, obviously trying to warm himself up. Their gloves helped but didn't completely keep out the cold. "I think so. The drug dealers are pretty far away from us now, and there isn't much of a moon, so I don't think they'll see the smoke. What I don't know is whether or not there's enough air moving around in here. I don't want us to die from carbon monoxide poisoning." He pulled a blue bandanna from his pocket, unfolded it and held the fabric loosely in different places around the cave, watching it move slightly in the different locations with the light from the flashlight. "Looks like there is some wind blowing through here, and it's moving from the back of the cave toward the entrance. See these crevices? That's where the air seems to be coming from. This cave probably opens up even more a little farther back." He pocketed the bandanna again. "That's good. We can build our fire back here near the rear. This is a small room, so we don't need much of a blaze to heat the space. I didn't want to block our way out anyway, and if we keep our heads pointed toward the opening while we're sleeping, we should have plenty of oxygen."

She watched in amazement as he pulled a small baggie of dryer lint from his backpack, then arranged the wood and dry leaves in a pile that resembled a rat's nest. The next thing she knew, he had used a match and the dryer lint to get the small fire going.

Kevin was quick to move closer once the fire was burning. "How come there isn't much smoke?" he asked as he held out his hands above the small flame.

"Because this is ash wood. I found a tree nearby that had lost a couple of branches. Ash wood is really dense and burns hot and longer than a lot of other woods. After a short time, these flames will disappear and the fire will be a smoldering bed of embers that should keep us warm throughout the night with hardly any smoke at all."

"That's so cool! How did you learn that?"

"Boy Scouts. We got to go camping sometimes, and I seemed to pull fire duty a lot. Apparently, the other guys thought it was a good idea to make sure I wasn't the one cooking the food." He leaned closer to Kevin and whispered, "I tend to burn things when I cook."

"I'd take burned food over nothing," Flynn said dryly as she also moved closer to the fire. "But we are not without resources. Although steaks and s'mores aren't on the menu, looks like tonight we're having oatmeal cream pies and Gatorade, thanks to Kevin here, who had the good sense to bring some food with him on our excursion." She gave him a smile. "We should probably save these granola bars for breakfast."

"That works," Derek agreed.

There were four of the soft oatmeal cookies, each individually wrapped in plastic. She passed them each one, then took the fourth and divided it into three equal pieces. "Okay, you two get to choose which parts of the cookie you want first. With Erin and me, the rule was always one person divides the food and the other gets to choose."

"Hey, that's a good rule!" Kevin agreed.

Flynn rubbed her hands together and put them even closer to the flames. She was still amazed that Derek carried dryer lint with him as a fire starter. Derek had saved some in a small Ziploc bag that he'd retrieved from the helicopter before they'd made their escape, and she was now starting to feel warm for the first time since the helicopter had been shot down.

After they finished their cookies and had passed around the Gatorade, the three of them went through the rest of their meager supplies in whispered tones. Kevin had managed to drop his bag of Gatorade and treats into the snow before climbing down the cliff, and miraculously, the bag was still intact and he'd remembered to retrieve it before they'd escaped into the woods. Derek and Flynn also had their cell phones, but of course, there was no service in this remote area of Colorado. They powered them down for now, hoping to save the battery power for a later date when they had a better chance of being able to reach someone.

Derek's navy backpack also contained a small survival kit with a thirteen-ounce pouch of peanut butter, a first aid kit, a small box of waterproof matches with the dryer lint, fishing line and hooks, and a Swiss Army knife. The kit also held an emergency blanket made out of Mylar polyester that Kevin had wrapped around his shoulders. The blanket was great for retaining body heat, even though the lightweight, waterproof material seemed like a flimsy piece of silver plastic wrap. Thankfully, Derek also had a small roll of toilet paper.

Flynn left the cave to use the bathroom, moving quietly to make sure they were still alone. There wasn't much light to see by, but she had enough to maneuver. She filled the empty Gatorade bottle with snow while she was out and brought it back in the cave with her when she returned, being careful to brush away any evidence that she had walked in the area. Hopefully, the snow would melt and keep them from getting dehydrated. She knew that in cold weather it was hard to know how much water her body was losing, especially when she was being active. On top of that, she didn't feel thirsty, which was often the case during the winter, even though she knew from her law enforcement training that after so much strenuous movement, her body fluids needed to be replenished. She might be a Florida girl, but she knew that eating snow was a bad idea and could really do more harm than good—the body had to use a lot of extra energy to warm up the cold snow. But she hoped that by melting the snow first and drinking the water, it would help.

Besides, at this point, they didn't have many alternatives.

When she pulled herself back into the cave, she noticed that Kevin had curled into a ball near the fire and was once again asleep. She dropped down wearily beside him, then looked over at Derek, who had rested his arms on his knees. His eyes were closed, but she doubted he was sleeping. "Did you learn anything when you were out and about?" she asked softly.

Derek slowly raised his head, then watched the firelight dance in Flynn's eyes. Despite the danger they were in, he couldn't help being thankful that she was back in his life. Several of her curls had gotten free from her blue headband, and while he watched, she pulled it loose, rearranged her hair and replaced the band, securing the strands away from her face.

The effect was mesmerizing. She was so beautiful, especially in the firelight. He couldn't believe he had pushed her away and slammed the door on their relationship so many years ago. Her skin was like creamy white porcelain, and the small brown freckles scattered across her nose gave her a youthful appearance that would never fade. She was cute and sweet like the girl next door, and her innocent appearance made her approachable and appealing.

Her inner beauty was just as hypnotic. Flynn was the most caring person he had ever met, and her forgiveness of his past actions was just more proof that she was a diamond that he should have treasured, not tossed aside. Yet even as the ice started to thaw from around his heart, he couldn't imagine that a relationship with her would ever be possible again, even though they were both single and unattached. That ship had sailed. But maybe, just maybe, now that they had cleared the air a bit between them, they could be friends as they worked together to survive this ordeal.

"I got close enough to hear some of them talking. They mentioned a man's name, and they might have been talking about Adam Cary. He's the one that I bought the helicopter business from when I got out of the army. I don't know him well, but he's wealthy and powerful and moved in important circles down in Breckenridge. I thought he moved to Denver, but I must be wrong. Or maybe he just told people that so he could operate more under the radar. In any case, he used to own a vacation rental company called Bear Creek. I don't know if he still does or not, but that might explain how he's able to keep his drug operation under wraps. Maybe he uses that company to launder his money or as a front for his illegal activities."

Flynn leaned forward, her expression animated. "Bear Creek was written on some of Erin's notes that I found in her apartment. I didn't know what it meant at the time. This is great information! If you're right and he's our drug lord, we may have just put a name and face to our enemy."

"There's more," Derek said quietly. "They mentioned a woman cop."

Flynn narrowed her eyes. "Did they say they shot her?"

Derek nodded. "Somebody from their organization did. I wouldn't be surprised if your sister found out about the drug trafficking and they shot her to take her out. It seems like they are hot to kill anyone that might stand in the way of their profits." He shifted. "I have to admit, they've done an admirable job of keeping their operation under wraps. Adam Cary is a powerful man who appears to be a wealthy and successful businessman— nothing more. He's well-liked and has an excellent reputation. If he is behind all this, the news is going to shock a lot of people."

Flynn ruminated on the information. "I'm not even sure Erin knew what she had discovered, but it could have been one of those cases where she was just starting to put the pieces together. Sometimes you don't know what you know or how it fits into the bigger picture until the evidence comes together. Her notes weren't that clear. She didn't mention Adam Cary, but maybe she hadn't gotten that far along in her investigation yet, and until she wakes up, I won't be able to ask her."

Derek nodded. "Well, she was certainly on the right track, and her digging must have scared Cary enough to want to put an end to her investigation. Without her pointing us in Cary's direction, who knows how long he would have continued getting away with his crimes? Now, once we get back into town, we have a real chance of stopping them." He poked at the fire with a small stick. There was basically just a bed of embers now, but they did a wonderful job of heating the small space.

He reached over and tucked the silver blanket closer to Kevin's sleeping body.

"You're good with him," Flynn whispered.

Derek laughed. He couldn't help himself. "I am not."

Flynn raised an eyebrow. "I'm not kidding. You'll make a great dad someday."

The thought terrified him. He thought back to images of his father and the pain he had endured at his father's hand. "I'm horrible with children. I don't have the patience."

"Says who?"

"Says me."

Flynn tilted her head, a look of surprise on her face. "I hope you change your mind someday. Just because your dad was a nightmare doesn't mean you don't have the heart and ability to take care of children. I know you, remember? And I know you'll make a good dad whenever the time comes. If it comes." She nodded toward the cave entrance before he had a chance to argue with her. "I'll take first watch. Why don't you get some sleep?"

He smiled at her. That was the second time she'd reminded him that she knew him to be a good person. He let that thought wash over him. It felt good. "I'm too tired to argue with you. Wake me up in a couple of hours and I'll relieve you."

"Deal."

He stretched out by the fire and pillowed his head on his arm, and another piece of ice melted from around his heart.

EIGHT

The buzzing seemed to get louder.

Flynn shook her head, but the pulsating mechanical sound didn't go away. She rubbed the sleep out of her eyes and looked across in the dim light at Kevin, who was swirling the Gatorade bottle over the fire embers, melting more snow into drinkable water. He smiled at her, and the peace she saw in his eyes warmed her heart. The sleep must have really rejuvenated him, and she said a silent prayer of thanks. She hadn't seen Kevin smile at all since she had arrived in Colorado, which hadn't surprised her, given the circumstances. Still, she welcomed the sight. The coals glowed softly, and the cave still held a wonderful warmth that made her feel rested and peaceful herself. She'd only had a few hours of sleep since she and Derek had traded off keeping watch during the night, but the rest had been enough to help her feel refreshed and ready to take on the new day.

The buzzing still didn't stop. Her brain clicked, and she finally recognized the sound. "Do you hear that?" she asked as she pulled herself up into a sitting position and then moved toward the entrance.

Kevin shrugged, not understanding. He took a drink

from the bottle, then spun it some more. "Yeah. So?" She didn't take the time to explain but instead glanced around quickly in the dim light and noticed Derek's absence. On hands and knees she pulled herself outside, looking for enemies as she did so. Derek was standing outside in the early morning light, squinting at the sky.

"Can you see it?" he asked, keeping his voice low.

"Nope, but I can hear the engine," Flynn said with a grin. "Search and rescue plane?"

Derek nodded, but he looked anything but happy. "That's my guess. I didn't file a flight plan because the FAA doesn't require it when we fly with visual instead of instrument flight rules, but my staff knows we never came home last night, and they knew we were going to check out those coordinates you found in your sister's apartment. I'm sure they called our disappearance in to law enforcement."

"You don't look too pleased."

"I'm not," Derek replied, still keeping his tone soft. "The dealers are going to be looking for us even harder now and wanting to make sure they catch us before the rescuers find us. And the odds of us safely signaling the folks in that plane up there are pretty low." He ran his hands through his hair. "So, we have more danger, not less. That search party is going to make getting down this mountain even harder."

She nodded. "I hadn't thought of it that way." She pulled her headband off, ran her fingers through her own hair and then replaced it, trying to tame her unruly curls. What she wouldn't give for a hairbrush! She grimaced and ran her tongue over her teeth. And a toothbrush. She sighed. Oh, well. There was no use wishing for the impossible. "What's our next move?"

Derek quirked an eyebrow. "You're the big detective. I'll let you decide." His expression showed that he was joking, but she recognized a bit of truth in his words. She liked being in control of her own investigations and usually enjoyed taking the lead if the opportunity presented itself or she was offered the chance. In this situation, however, she was happy to let Derek be in charge. She was definitely a city girl at heart, and not an outdoorswoman. "I'm a Florida girl, Derek. I can get you to the beach and back in a hundred-degree weather when the bridges are closed and show you were to find the spiny lobster in season, but these mountains and snowy conditions are your specialty, not mine." She gave him a wink and was happy that he was relaxing enough to tease her. In that small expression, she saw a piece of the Derek she had known back in college, when he had been happy and much more carefree.

She stretched a little, then stopped herself, hoping that their enemies were nowhere close by. Sound traveled farther than she thought, so she was purposefully keeping her voice low, but movement was also visible from a great distance, and the last thing she wanted to do was give away their position. Maybe she wasn't as awake as she thought.

She met Derek's eye, and her heart jumped. His beard and strong jaw made him look roguish and even more attractive in the morning light, and his dark blue eyes were watching her closely and shooting electricity across the small space that separated them. Memories flooded her of the many good times when they'd been dating back in the old days. She remembered talking for hours, walking hand in hand, and the softness of his lips. She recalled laughing at his jokes and cheering for him when he pitched softball in the church league. He had been her best friend. She missed the closeness they had shared.

What was wrong with her? They were fighting for their lives, and here she was reliving romantic thoughts from the past. She ruthlessly pushed the memories away. She was not getting back together with Derek, and recalling the past, even the good parts, was pointless. They'd had their chance to make it as a couple, and the relationship had crashed and burned before it had truly matured. Besides, she did not need or want a man in her life anymore. Hadn't she made that resolution after Ted had slammed the door on their relationship? What she did need was to focus on the here and now and keeping Kevin safe. That was all that mattered. Once they were back in civilization, then she could move on to solving her sister's shooting. There was no room for anything or anyone else in her life. "I'll take care of the fire," she said a little awkwardly and hurried back into the cave.

Flynn doused the embers with sand and packed up their meager supplies, then she and Kevin went outside with Derek, divided up the granola bars and passed around the Gatorade bottle. A grimness settled over the group, and the lighthearted atmosphere that had enveloped them only moments before dissipated like a fine mist. Survival and the trek ahead of them took precedence over all else. One way or another, they had to get down this mountain and to the police station with the evidence Flynn carried in her glove. Proving what they'd seen was the only way they could stop Adam Cary from continuing to manufacture and peddle his drugs.

After they drank all the water, Derek filled the bottle with snow again, then secured it in the backpack with the other items. He wasn't sure if the snow would melt during the trek, but it was worth the chance and didn't add much weight to his backpack.

Wordlessly, he set off with Kevin close behind him and Flynn in the rear. The sun's rays struggled to pierce the thick clouds and tree branches, but Derek was thankful for the overcast conditions. A storm had come during the night and dropped more snow on the mountain, and he predicted it would snow again later in the day. Hopefully the bad weather would send the search team home and would ultimately also make it harder on their pursuers. Of course, it would make it harder on them, too, but if it started snowing, the powder would cover their tracks and make it even tougher for the men with guns to discover their location.

They paused and rested twice before noon, and since the snow did indeed melt in the Gatorade bottle as they traveled, they were able to stop at times and take a drink and then refill the bottle with more snow. Even so, Derek wasn't sure they were getting enough hydration, even though the night before they had melted a copious amount of snow over the fire and drunk plentifully over and over again.

A little after lunchtime, the sky darkened and the heavy clouds began dropping fat white snowflakes. The three found a low-lying bush and huddled beneath the branches, and Derek pulled out the peanut butter. He was thankful the three of them were all mindful, including Kevin, of the need to share and make sure everyone got some of their precious food supplies. The peanut butter was the end of their rations, but he was grateful he'd kept the packet in his survival kit.

"Sure wish we had some crusty bread to go with that," Flynn said as she watched Derek squeeze some into his mouth.

"And some strawberry jam!" Kevin added as he took the silver pouch. Just as he was about to pinch some of the gooey butter into his mouth, they heard voices not far away.

"I saw movement over here. I'm sure of it!"

The man's voice instantly sent adrenaline throughout Derek's body, and he reached for his weapon and pulled the gun slowly out of his pocket. Flynn and Kevin both froze like statues, their eyes on him, looking for guidance.

About thirty feet away, a man in a dark green jacket came into view. He was wearing a black skull cap and carried a high-powered rifle in his gloved hands. He was struggling through the snow but heading right for them.

Derek had been in charge of his helicopter crew in the military and had been in a leadership role in several situations during his time in the service, but for some reason, the weight of responsibility he felt now with Flynn and Kevin at his side seemed almost tripled. Both Flynn and her nephew looked at him with such trust in their eyes that fear tightened a knot in his stomach. He *had* to keep them safe. There was no other option. He motioned for them to get down, and the three huddled behind the bushes and brush. Then he said a silent prayer, asking for God to protect them and hide them from the eyes of their pursuers.

"Wait for me," another man yelled, suddenly appearing behind the first. He was wearing a red parka, and while he also had a rifle, his was slung on his back. In his gloved hand, he carried a small set of binoculars. "Are you sure you really saw something?"

Even as the man's words drifted across the wooded area, the snow swirled and seemed to come down even harder than before, and a brisk wind suddenly buffeted them with a chilling yet obfuscating blast of snow, dried leaves and cold air.

The first man stopped about ten feet away from them, but it was obvious from his disoriented expression that he had lost sight of whatever he had thought he'd seen. "Who knows. This storm is picking up. I don't even care if we find them now. I just want a hot mug of coffee and a warm blanket. This is crazy!"

Derek had pulled his weapon, and he kept his finger near the trigger, just in case. He could hear his heart pounding in his ears. He never wanted to fire his gun at a human target, especially not with a child nearby to witness the carnage, but he would do so if forced. He prayed fervently that the two men wouldn't discover their hiding place and would leave them unscathed.

The second man stopped by the first, pocketed the binoculars and rubbed his gloved hands together. He glanced around the area but didn't look down or even in the general direction of where the three were huddled under the bush. Then he worked a glove off his hand with his teeth, pulled out his phone and punched some buttons. "Good grief. No service. There's no service anywhere up here on this mountain! How are we supposed to communicate when these stupid things hardly ever work!"

"How should I know? Let's head back to the rendezvous site." The man in the green coat started heading west, not waiting to see if the other man followed. The man with the phone shrugged, then stored his phone, put his glove back on and followed him away from the area.

Flynn let out a breath, and the moist air left a cloud around her mouth. Derek noticed and then looked away, his own breath slowly returning to normal. Against his own volition, his eyes returned to her lips, then rose to the pink flush in her cheeks. A warmth filled him that he didn't expect, and another surge of protectiveness swept over him.

"That was a close one," he whispered. She nodded and pulled Kevin close, then actually leaned against him. Derek held his breath, surprised yet enjoying the contact. It was the first time she'd touched him of her own volition since he'd seen her walking toward his helicopter on the tarmac. The weight of her felt good against his shoulder and made him feel special and trusted.

He thought about that for a minute. Flynn had always been someone who craved human touch. It was one of her primary love languages. She had always enjoyed snuggling on the couch and watching a movie or walking hand in hand around a duck pond. When he had tried to date after he'd left Flynn behind, that was one of the biggest things he missed about her presence. Now she avoided touch and seemed to stiffen whenever he was close. His mind returned to some of the other things he missed as well, like her laugh and her easy smile. He'd never enjoyed the company of other women the way he had felt totally at ease with Flynn. She had been his best friend…and had stolen his heart.

And he had walked away from her.

No, he had run away. And why? Because he was afraid of commitment. Because he was afraid he wasn't cut out to be a husband and a dad. And he had left horrible scars…on both of them.

But had anything really changed in his life since he'd made that decision? He was still afraid of having a family. He didn't want to imitate his father—a man who had always selfishly put his own needs above the wants and needs of his wife and son. Everything had revolved around him. No one else's opinion had ever mattered or even factored into the equation. His mother had slowly turned into an unhappy shell of a woman right before his eyes, and he couldn't stand it if he did the same thing to Flynn.

But would he have followed in his father's footsteps?

Flynn didn't think so.

Flynn thought he was a good person. She thought he would make a good dad. And the more time they spent together, the more her opinion of him mattered and bolstered his confidence in his personal failings. Maybe he could make different decisions…

They waited a full ten minutes in the same location as he ruminated on the past. Finally, Flynn squeezed his arm and he pulled himself out of the thoughts and memories that had overtaken him. "Should we go?"

"We should." He nodded. They pulled themselves out of the small enclave where they had been hiding and continued their trek down the mountain, but after only a few minutes, Flynn came up next to him and gently grabbed his arm.

"This snow is getting thicker, and the wind is really blowing. I don't think we can go much farther today. What do you think?"

He stopped and then glanced around them. Kevin looked like he was about to collapse, and Flynn had lines of exhaustion around her mouth and eyes. The snow was pretty deep here, and they were making very little progress. The only good news was that the snow was covering their tracks almost as quickly as they made them.

"Okay, let's go just a little farther and see if we can find some sort of shelter." He shielded his eyes from the wind and looked hard at his surroundings. There wasn't much beyond trees and small boulders, and he suddenly realized just how blessed they had been to find the cave the night before. Today, he didn't see anything similar that would protect them from freezing to death. It was time to get creative, and he immediately started working on a plan and sorting through different options.

Flynn nodded and fell back behind Kevin again, and they walked for another half an hour or so without finding any place that Derek felt would adequately protect them during the night from the cold and the building storm.

Had they survived the helicopter crash and being chased by gunmen only to freeze to death out here in the swirling snow?

NINE

Derek watched as Kevin took another step, then sank to his knees, unable to go any farther. He'd been dragging the last part of the hour anyway, but it was now obvious he just couldn't go on. They needed a solution, and they needed one fast. Derek studied the surrounding area, then came up with an idea. People used igloos as winter decorations, but they had been a real housing option for the Eskimos, or Inuit people, who had once used the shelters to survive the brutal Canadian winters. Americans had been using something similar for years—a snow cave. He'd heard about them but never constructed one. Could he make a cave out of snow that would have the same basic thermal properties as an igloo? After all, igloos were particularly effective at providing protection from freezing temperatures and high winds, so he assumed a snow cave would be about the same.

He glanced around the area once again. There weren't any other options. He'd never made a snow cave before, but it was time to do some fast out-of-the-box thinking if they were going to survive the night.

He motioned to Flynn, who had helped Kevin get back on his feet, then waited for her to come up by his side before broaching the idea. "I think we're done walking, but I don't see any sort of shelter out here from this storm, and the weather is only going to get worse."

"Yeah, I noticed the same thing," Flynn agreed. "Got any ideas?"

Derek nodded. "Actually, I do. I think we can make a snow cave. Building a shelter like that may be our only shot at surviving until morning. The temperature is dropping fast. I think we need to start building one now."

Flynn shrugged. "Sounds like a plan to me, but I've never made a snow cave. The only thing I've ever done is make a snowman, and that was when I was a kid. I don't have the first clue how to start. How do we do it?"

"First we find the right spot. Let's keep walking, and I'll let you know when I see what I'm looking for."

After about another fifteen minutes, Derek finally spotted an area that he thought might work for what he envisioned. Near the edge of a crop of rocks, there was a steep slope with a large buildup of snow already piled up against it. That mound of snow would be an excellent start and would save them valuable time since it was already several feet thick. The area was also heavily wooded, which would help eliminate some of the wind that was picking up.

"This will do," he said to Flynn, motioning with his hand. He glanced over at Kevin. "Kevin, just hang on for a little bit more. Your aunt and I are going to build you a really cool cave. Just wait. You're going to have an amazing story to tell your friends."

"Like Batman?" he asked hopefully, his teeth chattering. His eyes were red-rimmed and his lips were chapping, but the idea of living like a superhero sparked at least a bit of excitement and his brown eyes sparkled despite his weariness.

"Not exactly, but I'll see what I can do," Derek quipped.

He glanced around him and found a large piece of wood that resembled the head of a garden shovel, then got down on his hands and knees and started digging into the snow. "The entrance will be here, but it has to be below the main space where we're going to stay so the warm air will rise and stay in the cave with us. We can dig slightly upward here, see? Then we'll go more horizontally into this slope of snow when we get a couple of feet up. It looks like the snow is about six or seven feet deep here, so this ought to work perfectly."

Flynn raised her eyebrow but didn't comment. Instead, she found a similarly shaped piece of wood and started digging beside him. "Whatever you say, Balto."

"Balto?"

"Wasn't he a famous sled dog from way back when?"

Derek laughed. "I have absolutely no idea."

"Yeah, okay. Well, I'm a little short on jokes about famous creatures that have survived in the snowy wilderness. I'll try to come up with a few while we see if this snow cave idea of yours works." She smiled, and once again, her expression warmed him.

The snow was perfect for what he had envisioned, and thankfully, they didn't come across any large rocks or ice that would prevent the construction as they worked. The entrance was protected from the wind, and the angle allowed them to kick the displaced snow out behind them as they created the cave. The entrance tunnel was quickly complete and ended up being only a little wider than the space they need to crawl on their hands and knees. By the time they started working on the main chamber that would hold the three of them and give them a place to sleep, Kevin was a tad revived and was able to help with removing the snow they were shifting from the inside.

"Sure wish I had a real shovel," Flynn said under her breath as they pushed another load of snow behind them for Kevin to pull out. She leaned back for a moment and took a moment to catch her breath.

"What fun would that be?" Derek jibed. He winked at her, noticing her pink cheeks and vibrant red lips that were flushed from exertion. She sure was beautiful, even with the lines of strain and stress that painted her features. In fact, in his eyes, she was the most gorgeous woman on the planet. Who else would be working so diligently by his side, never giving up? He had to admit, they made a formidable team. He turned back to the snowy cave wall and continued digging.

Two and a half hours later, they were still excavating and tunneling in the cave, and Flynn and Derek started taking turns with one doing the digging and one removing the excess snow so they could each have a bit of time to rest. Kevin had taken refuge under a log and passed out, but before sleeping he had packed the snow tightly around the edges of their new home, giving their walls more stability.

Finally, Derek declared their new domicile complete. The walls and roof were a little over a foot thick, and they had constructed a pit of sorts that ran the length of the front of the cave that was deeper than the cave floor. This would allow a place for the colder air to go as the warmer air rose. The room wasn't large, but it was big enough for the three of them to sit up, lie down and stretch out a bit without being cramped. They also smoothed the inside roof and walls of the cave as much as possible with their gloves to prevent dripping. As an extra precaution, Derek, used a stick to carve grooves in the walls for the water to run down, just in case dripping did occur if their body heat managed to melt some of the interior.

Flynn woke Kevin with a gentle shake. "We're done. Want to come take a look?"

Kevin sat up and rubbed the sleep out of his eyes. "Can we close the cave all up and start a fire?"

"No," Derek replied, still keeping his voice low in case the perpetrators were anywhere close. "But we really won't need one. Our body heat will keep the small space nice and cozy while we're in there." He brushed some snow off his shoulder. "We couldn't use a fire anyway. Fires take up a lot of oxygen, and we want to be able to breathe without a problem. We have to leave at least part of the entrance open, too, to make sure we get enough air circulation." He motioned toward the forest. "Can you find me a stick about an inch thick and about three feet long out there?"

"Sure," Kevin said, apparently glad to feel useful. He pulled himself up and quickly disappeared into the nearby stand of trees, apparently rejuvenated by his nap. Despite the wind and snow, he came back shortly with a stick just a bit smaller than a baseball bat. "How about this?"

"I think it will work," Derek replied with a small smile. He broke off the extra branches, then used the long stick to create a slanted hole in the roof of the structure, right through the snow.

"Why'd you just put a hole in the ceiling?" Kevin asked. "Isn't that going to let out all of our warm air?"

"Like I was saying, we need to make sure we have enough air to breathe. This ventilation hole will let air in from the top. We will lose a little bit of the warm air, but it will also help make sure we don't suffocate during the night, and that is really important." He glanced around at the surrounding snow that was already piling up around them and doing a fairly adequate job of camouflaging their new cave, and all the footprints they'd made. Still, he wanted a bit more, just in case someone happened upon them. As far as they knew, the drug dealers were still out canvassing the area, despite the worsening weather. He didn't want to be sloppy and give away any clues about their whereabouts.

"Let's all use the bathroom one last time, and when you come back, bring some extra pine straw with you and throw it around the area so this place looks more natural, okay?"

They complied, and once Derek was satisfied with the result, they crawled inside the structure. The inside room was much smaller than the rock cave where they'd spent the previous evening. In fact, the entire area was only about as big as a Jacuzzi, but the space was sufficient for their needs, and Derek was extremely thankful he'd even heard about snow caves and knew the basics of building one. He was no expert, but the result of their labor would probably save their lives.

"Are you sure we don't need a fire?" Kevin asked as soon as they were settled. "I'm still really cold." They had brought in quite a bit of pine straw to keep themselves from having to lie directly on the snow, and Kevin was quick to pull out the thermal Mylar blanket again from the backpack and lay the fabric over the pine straw. It wasn't a fancy billet, but the makeshift bed would do for the night.

"I promise we won't need one, and the flames would only melt the cave anyway," Derek responded. He pushed the backpack over near the entrance but left plenty of room for air to pass by and was careful not to block the trench that the cooler air needed to escape. He also pulled out the Gatorade bottle, drank his fill after offering a drink to the others and then refilled the container with snow from the lower wall near the entrance. He didn't know how warm it would actually get inside their homemade cave and if the temperature would be sufficient to melt the snow in the bottle, but so far, they had been able to consume adequate water without suffering dehydration.

By the time he leaned back, Flynn was already lying supine and had placed Kevin between them. To his own surprise, the room was already getting warm. He felt a small breeze coming in through the hole he'd put in the ceiling but didn't put anything over the opening to block it. He wanted that air coming in to make sure they had good ventilation throughout the night.

"Got any more of that peanut butter left, champ?"

Kevin shook his head. "Nope. But I'm so tired, I'm having a hard time even thinking about food right now." The boy snuggled up to Derek, and although Derek stiffened at the contact, after a few minutes, he finally started to relax and allowed the closeness. Children had always made him uncomfortable, but with everything else they had been dealing with lately, it was hard to stress about his hang-ups, and he didn't want to push the boy away. After a few more minutes, Kevin's breathing evened out and he was once again asleep. To Derek's own surprise, after he was past his initial trepidation, he realized he was actually starting to enjoy having the boy near him. The kid needed guidance, and he found himself wanting to protect Kevin and help him, almost as much as he wanted to take care of Flynn. The feeling was odd and unexpected, yet he found the emotion strangely satisfying.

"Is he out?" Derek finally asked, wanting to make sure so he didn't move the wrong way and wake him up unnecessarily.

"Seems so," Flynn replied quietly. "You did a great job with him today. He'll remember building this snow cave with you for the rest of his life."

Derek let that idea sit for a minute or two before commenting. "It was a fun project, but more importantly, it will probably save us from freezing." He sighed. "I have a lot more respect for the Eskimos now. Who knew a snow cave took so long to build, though? Putting it together was a lot more work than I expected, too, but well worth it if it means we'll make it till tomorrow."

Flynn laughed softly. "You mean they didn't mention the time and effort requirements in the article you read in some outdoor explorer magazine?"

Derek had initially been lying on his back, but he slowly rolled to his side so he could face Flynn and see her expressions. He was careful not to wake Kevin, who stayed sandwiched between them. With a click, Derek turned on his small flashlight and made the light reflect off the back of the cave so he could see Flynn's face better. Her visage was still steeped in shadows, but he had enough light to make out her beautiful blue eyes and the peaceful expression painted across her features, which made her even more beautiful than she'd seemed before. She had to be exhausted, and armed men were trying to track her down and kill her, but she hadn't complained once. She just kept going, like the Energizer Bunny, and managed to keep a positive attitude no matter what the circumstances. She was an inspiration. "Nope. I have no idea if I constructed this cave properly. I haven't read any articles about it. Let's hope our attempt works out as well as I planned."

"You're amazing, you know that? I never would have even thought of such an idea."

He didn't reply, and for a few minutes, he just looked at her and let those words soak in for a moment. Amazing? Really? She was serious—he could see admiration in her expression—but he didn't want to accept the compliment. She was the amazing one. He didn't think he was amazing at all. In fact, his years on Earth seemed to be a series of horrible, life-changing mistakes, one right after another. Finally, he had to respond and deny her words. "There's nothing amazing about me. Anyone can build a snow cave. Even a Florida girl."

Flynn laughed again, then reached across Kevin and gave Derek a playful nudge. "Not this one. I don't have the first clue about how to build a snow cave, and I certainly wouldn't have known to make the entrance at an angle like that and build a trench in the front so the cold air can have a place to go. That's pure genius."

She paused for a moment and scrutinized his face. For some reason, she felt a desire to touch his cheek and encourage him, and she started to reach for him, but at the last second, she let her hand fall without doing so. She was afraid to touch him—afraid that if she did, her heart would get engaged and she would once again open herself up to hurt when he walked away after this was over. And he *would* walk away. It was a guarantee. He'd done it before, and he would do it again. Still, she could encourage him without opening herself up. It was the least she could do after everything he had done for them. "If you hadn't been our pilot, who knows what would have happened to us? And by the way, you were excellent with Kevin tonight. The poor kid was exhausted, but you gave him time to rest and then let him help with the building once he got his second wind. It really made him feel like he was contributing."

Derek paused a moment, apparently considering her words. "He's doing incredibly well."

"He's only eleven years old."

"He's pretty smart for a kid that age." Derek propped his head up on his hand. "I mean, I don't know many kids, but he seems to be a fast thinker."

"Yeah, Erin is really proud of him. She says a lot of times, Kevin is the one that comes up with the best ideas, and she forgets he's only eleven." Her thoughts turned to everything they had been through today. She was exhausted, both mentally and physically, yet she also felt an inner peace. Despite all that had happened, they had survived another day. "You know, I think God really protected us earlier when those shooters walked up on us. I mean, we were right there, only a few feet away from them, and they never saw us. And then that wind and snow started really coming down and camouflaged us even better—and just in the nick of time. It was great."

Derek nodded slightly. "I agree."

"Back in college, we used to go to church every Sunday together, but I have to admit, I haven't been attending like I used to. Unfortunately, I have to work a lot of weekends, but I need to make more of an effort and find something that will fit into my schedule regardless." She motioned with her hand. "Do you still go?"

"Not as much as I should," Derek admitted quietly.

Flynn grimaced. "I regret falling away. This trip is proof of how much I need God in my life." She paused a moment, thinking through old conversations she'd had with her sister. "You know, Erin's husband wouldn't let her go to church, or take Kevin, and I think even though he left them about a year ago, she struggled with going back, even though her ex is not in their lives anymore controlling their every move. I hope I can talk to her about her faith when she's healed up a bit and help them get plugged in somewhere in Frisco. Kevin and I have only talked about his beliefs a little so far, but I want to make sure I introduce him to Jesus really well before I go back to Florida."

Derek nodded. "That's a good idea. Maybe I'll go, too. I want to get reconnected, and sometimes it's easier to go with a friend. I don't know Erin very well, but it might be nice to see Kevin again after this is all over. It's obvious that God has been looking out for us this entire time. Without His help, we'd be dead by now for sure."

Flynn was shocked. She knew Derek struggled around children, even though they'd really never discussed why. He'd never wanted to talk much about his past and had quickly shut down the conversation any time she'd asked. Even so, here he was, considering helping her nephew out once they got back to the real world and out of this surreal life-or-death experience. "If you think about it, will you pray for Erin and Kevin?"

"You bet," Derek answered. "Finding a church home is important. I was already thinking about a few places that I'd like to visit."

Flynn let a moment pass, then another. She had so much to be thankful for in her life. She sighed, then murmured softly, "Have I told you how thankful I am that you're here with us? Although I am sorry to have involved you and put you in danger." She looked into his eyes and saw deep emotions there that surprised her. She quickly looked away.

"You didn't cause the danger we're in," Derek replied.

"Maybe not, but—"

"No buts," he interrupted. "There's no place I'd rather be than right here with you, right now."

Again, Flynn felt the desire to reach across and touch him, but she stopped herself a second time, even as electricity seemed to sizzle and crackle in the air. What was the point? They were renewing their friendship, and that was good. And there was definitely an attraction still bubbling between them. But that was it. Physical attraction. They'd already tried to have a meaningful relationship, and it just hadn't worked. When they reached civilization again, Derek would go his way and she would go hers.

So why did that idea make her feel even colder inside?

TEN

Flynn verified that the flash was turned off, then snapped a quick picture of the outside of their snow cave with her small camera. She'd taken a few shots of their expedition so far and hoped to share them with her sister to show off how well Kevin had done during the trip. Taking photos seemed kind of silly on some level, but she knew in her heart that they were going to make it, and someday, she'd want these pictures to prove how they had survived in such difficult circumstances.

Photography had been a hobby since she'd gotten her first digital camera when she was ten. Taking photos made her feel like herself, as if killers weren't actually chasing her, Kevin and Derek down the mountain.

She pocketed the camera, verified her pistol was still in her other pocket and the safety was engaged, and that the SD card with the photos of the crime scene was secured in her boot. All was well. With a quick last look around, she turned and followed Kevin and Derek, who were already moving slowly down the mountain.

She had no idea how much longer they were going to be walking through the snow, but the hunger was starting to catch up to her. They were now completely out of food and were burning tons of calories with their trek down the mountain. At least they had each managed to drink a fair amount of water before leaving the cave. Thankfully, they'd also all gotten a good night's sleep, and the rest and fluids had done quite a bit to revive all three of them. Derek and she had decided no one needed to stay up to keep watch, because the storm would probably keep their pursuers away during the night. Even if it didn't, the snow cave was hard to recognize as anything beyond an icy mound, and they both felt confident that they were safe—at least for the night.

Today, the weather had changed. Gone were the blistering cold wind and falling snow. This morning, the sun was shining and reflecting off the blanket of white that covered everything, and the brightness made everything look clean and fresh, despite their predicament. Snow covered the trees and fields, and the scene looked like a Christmas card. The landscape would have been a beautiful sight if she'd been on vacation. And she'd even seen a bright red fox in the distance, playing and jumping in the air. She was thankful that the wind had died down and the gray clouds had disappeared and been replaced by fluffy white puffs that dotted the blue sky. Hopefully, today they would make it back to civilization. They had to be getting close. Of course, if the weather made it easier for them, the clear skies also made it easier for their adversaries, and she was still very cognizant of the danger they faced. Still, what she wouldn't give for a good pair of sunglasses!

Sunglasses and a cheeseburger, she amended. And maybe a chocolate shake.

Flynn pulled out her cell phone and quickly checked

the screen. Still no service. The lack of a cell tower nearby didn't surprise her, but it did frustrate her. Every time she'd checked she'd had zero bars, and she was using up precious battery power with her constant checking.

She turned and looked carefully around her, then followed Kevin and Derek. She hadn't seen anyone following them, but she kept her eyes peeled as well. She was sure their pursuers would be doubling their efforts to find them today since the weather had cleared. She didn't want anyone sneaking up on her six, and keeping watch was the least she could do since Derek was tasked with leading them down the mountainside. He had enough to worry about, and if she could put her law enforcement skills to good use to keep them safe, then all the better.

The three of them continued through the snowy pass, keeping to the tree line as much as possible so their footprints wouldn't be so easy to see or follow. There were no new flakes coming down that would help disguise their path, and the snow was still thick from yesterday's storm, making the going difficult and slow, despite the sunshine that made it easier to see. Hunger gnawed at her stomach, but she pushed the pain away and kept going. She would eat well once she made it to a restaurant... the biggest carb-filled plate she could find. But first they would all have to make it to the buffet unscathed.

Derek suddenly stopped and pointed up ahead, then motioned for them to stay quiet.

She went forward a few more steps, then saw what he had made him stop. Off in the distance, still a mile or so away, she could just make out a mountain pond that had apparently frozen over.

But that wasn't the interesting part.

The best part was that on the other side of the pond, there was a small cabin, and smoke was swirling out of the chimney, almost as if the wisps were welcoming them home. Long icicles decorated the edges of the roof, and snow covered the roof in gentle piles and was even hanging off the edges in places. Talk about a picturesque image for a Christmas card!

Excitement surged through her. They were saved! Surely someone was in the cabin. She didn't see any vehicles parked outside, nor did she see any movement around the building. But even so, the smoke testified to the occupancy, and whoever was living there probably had food, water, a way to communicate with the rest of the world and even warmth to share. Her hunger and worry seemed to suddenly disappear, and all three of them started forward with new vigor and excitement in their steps.

Eventually they reached the edge of the frozen water, although they were still trying to be mindful of their surroundings. Derek motioned for them to stop as he surveyed the scene. The pond was rather large, about the size of a baseball diamond, and the way around seemed long and difficult through a lot of underbrush and woods.

"What are we waiting for? I'm starving! Somebody's got to have food in there," Kevin cried, and before either adult could stop him, he ran out onto the ice.

Flynn's heart was in her throat as she heard the boy's words and watched him run as if he was in slow motion. He had thrown caution to the wind, not only by the volume of his words, but also by the rash behavior that now had him slipping across the ice as his feet tried to gain purchase on the slippery surface.

Suddenly, a loud crack sounded across the pond, and the ice started to splinter like a giant crack in a windshield. The sound was so loud that some of the nearby trees shook, and snow fell from the heavily laden branches in puffs around the edge. Kevin suddenly stopped and looked back at his aunt, fear painted across his face as he realized his mistake. Their eyes locked, and he mouthed one solitary word.

"Sorry."

Flynn didn't hesitate. She ran after him, right across the ice, and dived for him just as the primary fracture reached his feet. Her hands pushed him back, hard, and the momentum sent him flying across the ice, landing on his rear end and sliding to safety well away from the crack that was opening beneath them.

Flynn didn't make out as well. The ice splintered under her feet, and the next thing she knew, she had fallen into the frigid pond and she was flailing, completely underwater. The temperature shocked her, and for a moment she couldn't move as the darkness and quiet muted her senses. Then the lack of air started to cause a searing pain in her chest, and she began desperately trying to swim back to the surface. Air bubbles swirled around her head, making it hard to see, and chunks of ice hampered her progress. Flynn could tell the surface was close above her, though, and she kicked madly with her legs, desperate for air in her lungs. Her arms started to feel heavy, as if she could barely move them, but quitting was not an option. With her last ounce of strength, Flynn pushed her head through to the air outside and gulped madly, her arms finally obeying her and moving to grab on to something, anything, that would keep her from going under again. Chunks of ice of all sizes surrounded her. Her lungs burned, and a mixture of air and water entered her mouth, chilling her insides even more.

Bits of her life suddenly flashed before her eyes like a slideshow. She saw her parents, her first dog, her sister and herself riding bikes down the street, and later, the two of them celebrating her college graduation. Then she saw Derek walking away from her without looking back, followed by her own promotion to the rank of detective...then everything went black.

Derek's heart tripled its beat as he watched in horror. This couldn't be happening. They couldn't have gone through everything that they had survived the last two days to die here in a frozen lake in the Colorado mountains. He had lost Jax. He couldn't— *He wouldn't lose Flynn!* His heart told him to run after her on the ice, but his head stopped him and made him take a few moments to design a plan. He gingerly put one foot on the ice, then another, and came from an angle to the hole in the ice, rather than following the same path Flynn and Kevin had taken. Despite the fear and anxiety flowing through his veins, he forced himself to move carefully, making sure the ice was firm underneath him before taking another step toward the shocking scene that was playing out in front of him. He couldn't help Flynn if he was also lost in the lake.

He took another step...then one more. He made steady progress and moved as quickly as he dared, even though everything inside him was telling him to run toward the hole in the ice where Flynn had fallen through. Would he be able to even see her, or would she be locked underneath the ice, unable to find the surface again in a watery grave?

When he got close to the opening in the ice, he quickly dropped to his knees on the sturdiest section he could find and bent over as far as he dared. Flynn's body was right below the water's surface, and her head kept popping up, searching for air. Her arms were reaching upward, and she was grasping at the ice around the edge of the hole, trying to pull herself out but unable to find something sturdy to hold on to or pull against. He reached for her under the chunks of ice and tried to grab her thrashing arms. It was tough at his angle, but he readjusted his body so he could reach even farther under the ledge of ice. Finally, he was able to secure one of her wrists, and he held it tightly, grasping her with every ounce of strength he possessed. Adrenaline and fear made him even stronger than normal, and he pulled as hard as he could, bringing her out from under the layers of ice and farther into the hole. Then he grabbed her other wrist so he had a firm grip on both of them. He tugged as hard as he could and as quickly as possible to get her out of the icy hole. She was incredibly heavy due to the water that had soaked her clothing, and he felt and heard the ice cracking under his own feet as he stood, picked her up off the ice and started making for the edge.

At the sound of another crack, he broke into a run, diving the last few feet and landing with Flynn in his arms on the bank of the lake in a pile of frozen snow and ice. He caught his breath, then quickly sat up and moved to her side. She was unresponsive. Her skin was pale, and her lips were blue. She had quit moving completely, and her eyes were closed and lifeless.

"Flynn!" He shook her but got no response. Panic and dread fought for supremacy as he rolled her to her side. Water and mucus dribbled out of her mouth and nose. He was about to roll her over on her back and start CPR when she suddenly started choking.

Relief, hot and heavy, swept over him from head to toe. "Oh God, thank You!" He pulled her into his arms and held her close for just a moment, then moved her quickly to her side so she could clear the remaining water from her system. "Flynn, I thought I'd lost you!" She continued to sputter and choke, but eventually, the spasms slowed and her breathing gradually improved. She raised up her gloved hand and touched his jaw, and they held each other for several minutes as she struggled to recover from the episode. Her body started shaking, and her teeth chattered.

Kevin stood a few steps away, his skin ashen. He was crying softly and shaking, and at one point, he covered his eyes with his sleeve. Derek noticed and reached out to him, beckoning with his hand. "Come here, Kevin." At first the boy stood frozen, as hard and unyielding as the ice that surrounded them, but after a moment he moved to Derek's side, each step filled with trepidation. Derek pulled the boy close as soon as he was within reach. "It's okay, Kevin. She's going to be okay."

"But she could have died..." he choked out.

"But she didn't. She's breathing now, and see? Her color is coming back," Derek reassured him. "After a while, she's going to be talking and laughing just like her old self."

The three of them stayed like that for a few minutes, but Derek knew they couldn't stay here much longer.

Flynn *would* die from hypothermia if they couldn't get her warmed up immediately. Thankfully, they were across the pond now, and the cabin was only a short distance away. "Okay. I need your help, okay? We've got to get her into that house and close to a fire." He slowly disengaged himself, then stood and lifted Flynn into his arms. With Kevin following closely behind him, he made his way to the cabin.

Despite his words of assurance to Kevin and Flynn's physical improvement, Derek was still scared that Flynn was going to die, just like Jax. Even though his brain told him he had reached her in time and she would be good as new once they got her warmed up, his heart was still fluttering with fear. The anxiety was almost incapacitating. Even so, he couldn't stop—he had to do everything in his power to help her survive. He carefully carried her up the stairs and asked Kevin to knock on the door. He wanted to shout out but dared not take a chance since he still didn't know if their enemies were near or not. For that matter, he didn't know if the person living in the cabin was friend or foe, but either way, he was about to find out.

Without that person's help and the warmth the fire offered, Flynn would surely die.

ELEVEN

The door opened slowly, and a man in his early seventies or so raised his bushy eyebrows when he saw the sight on his porch. Flynn didn't get a good look at him but didn't really care what he looked like as long as he let them inside. She was colder than she'd ever been in her life, and her entire body was racked with shivers that she couldn't control or stop. It was hard for her to think or even concentrate on anything beside the tremendous cold that seemed to permeate every cell of her body.

"She fell in the lake," Derek said simply. "Can we borrow your fire?"

"Of course! Bring her in, bring her in," the older man said quickly as he stepped out of the way. Derek turned so he could carry her through the doorway and carefully stepped over the threshold. Kevin followed them in, gripping the navy backpack that held their small stash of supplies tightly in his gloved hands. Once they were all inside, the older man shut the door behind them.

The living room space wasn't large, but had an open feel with a cathedral ceiling. The walls were made of logs, and it was rustically decorated with deer and moose prints and a theme of dark green accents. A large fireplace with a roaring fire was in the corner, and Derek hurried over and laid Flynn in front of the fire. He took off his own gloves and coat, then turned to Flynn and removed her coat, gloves and boots. The older man was quickly at his side and offering a stack of blankets, a T-shirt and sweatpants. All were clean and smelled sweetly of cedar chips. Derek covered Flynn up to protect her modesty, and while she huddled under a blanket, he helped her pull off her wet jeans and flannel shirt and put on the dry shirt and pants. The pants were a bit big, but they had a drawstring, and she tied up the waist tightly, then lay on the floor, exhausted. That small bit of effort was all she could manage. She didn't even think she could sit up by herself. All she wanted to do was fall asleep and not wake up until next week sometime.

She turned slightly as she watched Derek remove his boots. He left on the rest of his clothes, which had to be a bit damp in places, but he didn't seem to mind. Her eyes locked with his, and she could see the worry and fear still consuming him. He couldn't keep his eyes off her.

"Thank you," she said softly. "You saved my life."

"You're welcome," he said as he moved to kneel beside her. "I keep telling myself that you survived and you're going to be fine, but I don't think I've really accepted it yet." He gently pulled her hairband off and then pushed the wet hair back from her face. "Everything happened so fast. I don't think I've ever been more scared in my entire life. When I saw you go in that icy water…" He touched her cheek gently and then cupped her chin with his hand, even though she tensed. "I thought I had lost you."

He sat on the floor and leaned back against a nearby

couch, then pulled her into his arms so she was facing the fire with her back to his chest. She stiffened, but he didn't let go. He pulled the blankets with her and rearranged them around her. With gentle fingers, he massaged her arms and neck, bringing a warm tingling to her skin as the circulation returned. He took several deep breaths, and she could tell he was trying to slow his heartbeat and the panic that she could still feel beating strongly behind his ribs.

"I hope those clothes fit you okay," the older man said as he ambled up to the couch. "Are you doing better now?"

Flynn smiled and nodded, and Derek cleared his throat that was clogged with emotion. "You're a lifesaver, mister. I don't think she would have made it if you hadn't been here with your fire going. We owe you our lives."

The man tilted his head and looked embarrassed at the praise. "Anyone would do the same. But I'm happy to help."

Derek motioned with his head toward Kevin, who was still standing by the edge of the couch, looking a bit lost. "That's Kevin, my name is Derek and this is Flynn."

"I'm Lee Clark," the man responded. "Would you like some hot chocolate?"

"That would be wonderful," Derek said. "We haven't eaten today, so if you have any food, we would be very grateful if you could share some."

Lee raised his eyebrows but stood and didn't press for answers to the questions no doubt swirling in his head. "I'm sure there's a story there, but let's get you warm and fed before we do anything else." He looked toward Kevin. "Young man, why don't you take off your coat and stay awhile? I have those dining room chairs by the table over there. See them? How about you bring them over closer to the fire and spread out these wet clothes on them. That will probably help them dry faster."

Kevin nodded quickly and went to work, apparently happy to have something to do. While Lee rumbled around in the kitchen, Kevin took off his jacket and gloves and then brought over all the chairs and hung up the coats and wet clothing. Then he organized the boots so they were also closer to the flames.

A few minutes later, Lee came back over near the fire with a folded sheet tucked under his arm and a small serving tray laden with mugs and spoons. "I know you don't want to leave that fire, Ms. Flynn, so I think a picnic is in order."

He handed her a mug of steaming hot chocolate, and she wrapped her hands around the mug, letting the warmth seep into her skin. It was pure joy. She took a small sip, then another, letting the warm liquid slowly heat her from the inside out. Lee handed a second mug to Derek and a third to Kevin and then took his tray back into the kitchen. A few minutes later, he returned a second time with plates and silverware, and finally he came back again with mounds of food on two different platters. He laid out a spread that would have made a bed-and-breakfast jealous. There were stacks of pancakes, butter on a dish and a small pitcher of syrup, a plateful of scrambled eggs, and large slices of ham and crispy brown bacon.

Flynn let Derek make her a plate, and then she continued to lean against him as she started eating, having no shame as she dug hungrily into the plate of heaping food. She tried to move away to give him room to eat, too, but he held her gently in place. "Stay put. You need my body heat. It will help you warm up."

She wasn't sure about that, but she didn't want to argue. Being held by Derek helped her feel safe and secure for the first time since she had landed in Colorado. Yet the closeness they were sharing brought back memories of when they'd been a couple so many years ago, memories that were better off forgotten and were now a catalyst to making her feel lost and alone. There was something wrong with her—something that made men run in the opposite direction whenever they got too close. She didn't want to go through that heartache again. It was too painful. Derek's touch now made her feel vulnerable and unsure, even as the air seemed to sizzle with electricity that popped between them.

Did she want a man in her life? No, she did not. She had forsworn all relationships after her last one had ended so poorly. Derek and Ted had both said they loved her, and both had left her with deep emotional scars. She was fine on her own. She didn't need a man in her life. But she had to admit, she missed the closeness of having someone to share things with—both the good times and bad. She missed laughing together, the camaraderie, the knowledge that no matter how bad things got, someone had her back.

She missed Derek.

He had been the love of her life. No one else she had dated had even come close, not even Ted. She missed his kisses. She missed holding hands and snuggling during a movie.

But Derek had made it clear that he didn't want to be

with her. Sure, he was being nice and helping her. But he was doing these things because he was a good person, not because he had any romantic feelings for her. She was the one projecting and hoping for feelings that just didn't exist and apparently never would.

She sighed inwardly. The past was over and done. For now, she would enjoy the companionship he offered. It was enough. It would have to be.

Derek reached over to the platters and filled a plate for himself, then set it on the floor within arm's reach and fed himself with his right arm while holding her with his left. She glanced over at Kevin, who was also eating a large stack of pancakes and tucking into some eggs and ham as well. A feeling of utter contentment settled over her despite their dire circumstances, and once she had eaten, she gave up the battle and fell asleep right there in Derek's arms.

Lee noticed and motioned with his hands toward Flynn as he sipped meditatively on a mug of hot chocolate. "She's out. Falling in that water took a lot out of her." He stood and started clearing the dishes away. "Boy, you weren't kidding when you said you were hungry!"

"I'm sorry we put you to so much trouble..." Derek started, but Lee waved his words away.

"I think it's great! Reminds me of my younger days. I always loved cooking for the family. Makes me feel useful."

Derek started to move Flynn a bit so he could stand. "I'll help you out with the dishes..."

This time, Lee put up his hands in a motion to stop him. "You will not. What you will do, young man, is sit right there with that pretty woman and take care of her and let her rest. I can take care of these dishes myself. I've been doing dishes for years, and I'm an expert. No, the three of you need rest, and rest is what you're going to get."

Derek watched Lee go, then turned his attention to Flynn. He shifted a bit and adjusted her against him so that his muscles wouldn't cramp. She felt so warm and perfect in his arms, he felt like he could sit like this forever. He didn't have the words to really express all that he was feeling, but he could show her with his actions. He would make sure she was safe, no matter the cost.

He glanced over at Kevin. The boy was still sitting at the edge of the fireplace, his expression dejected and unhappy. He'd finally removed his boots and added them to the rest by the fire and periodically held up his hands so they were closer to the flames. His skin was red from sun and windburn and his lips were chapped, but otherwise, the boy looked healthy and had done amazingly well during their quest for survival. Still, Derek realized the episode at the lake would probably bother him for some time. Maybe he could help with that. He wasn't good with kids, but he had to at least try to smooth things over.

"Kevin, why don't you come closer and wrap up in that blanket?" He motioned toward a navy throw that lay in a heap by the fire.

The boy looked wary at first but slowly complied. Then he sat and wrapped the blanket around his thin shoulders and stared into the fire.

"How are you doing?" Derek asked.

"Okay," he responded, his voice low.

"Hmm. Well, we should probably talk about what happened at the lake, don't you think?"

Kevin shrugged. "I guess." He was quiet for a moment, and then Derek could hear his quiet sobs.

"Well, you made a mistake today, but I want you to know that I forgive you, and I'm sure Flynn does, too."

The boy stopped crying in surprise and made a hiccupping sound. "What? Really? I thought you'd be really mad at me. Don't you hate me now? I feel so guilty. Aunt Flynn got hurt and it's all my fault." He sniffled, found a stray napkin and blew his nose.

"No, Kevin. I'm not mad, and I don't hate you. Everyone makes mistakes."

"Not you," Kevin said, his eyes large. "I bet you never make mistakes."

Derek laughed. If this kid only knew… "I've made plenty, believe me. Some mistakes I've even made more than once." He shifted slightly. "In fact, all people make mistakes, but let me tell you a little secret. It's how we fix those mistakes that matters, and how we learn from them." He looked the boy in the eye. "You start by apologizing to the people who were hurt by your actions, and really mean it. And then you do your best to fix the mistake and try not to make the same mistake twice."

Kevin's eyes widened. "But you said you've made the same mistake more than once before."

"That's very true. And you know what? That's because none of us are perfect. We're all going to get it wrong sometimes, no matter how hard we try to get it right. And that's okay. It's our attitude and our hearts that matter. As long as you're doing your best, that's all we can ask of you. Just be sure to always do the best you can, and apologize if you get it wrong, and take responsibility for your mistakes. Then forgive yourself and move on. Sound like a good plan?"

"Yes, sir," the boy responded, a hopeful tone to his voice.

Derek reached over and pulled Kevin close with his right hand, letting the boy rest against him. Once again, he actually felt comfortable with the closeness, and he didn't shy away from the contact. The irony of his words wasn't lost on him. Here he was teaching this kid an important life lesson—a lesson he still hadn't learned himself.

Even though the military tribunal had cleared him of all wrongdoing, Derek had never really forgiven himself for being the pilot in the crash that had killed his friend. Had he done his best to save him? Yes, he had. He would never have intentionally hurt Jax, and he had done all in his power to do his job and protect the people who flew with him. Yet tragedy had still occurred, and he had been powerless to stop it. He needed to forgive himself and move on, just as he was trying to teach this young boy.

He hugged Kevin and Flynn, and felt another big piece of ice chip off his frozen heart. Maybe there was hope for him after all.

TWELVE

Flynn woke up a few hours later on the floor by the fire, still lying against Derek's chest with Kevin also huddled next to them. Heat still radiated from the flames, and the bone-deep chill that had invaded her body when she'd gone under the ice had finally subsided. She was beginning to feel like herself again, and even her stomach had quit complaining because she had eaten her fill of their host's wonderful breakfast.

She stretched slightly, and Derek must have felt it, because he woke as well. She'd hoped to slip away before he realized how long they'd been sitting together. She didn't want to make him feel awkward or uncomfortable by their closeness. "You make a pretty good pillow," she quipped as she sat up and quickly moved away from him. She scooted closer to the fire and stretched out her hands, soaking up the warmth. Why did she feel so chilled all of a sudden?

Derek glanced at Kevin, who was still sleeping against him, and gently shifted him so he was lying completely on the floor on a dark green braided rug. The boy didn't stir, even when Derek tucked the blanket around him. Derek stretched out his arm and rubbed his shoulder.

"Kid weighs a ton," he said lightly, but Flynn was sure she heard a pleased tone to his voice. She was glad he wasn't annoyed. Derek had always been good around children, even though he seemed to have a hard time realizing it. They'd rarely talked about it, and whenever she'd asked him about kids in the past, he'd changed the subject and refused to discuss his feelings. There was something there, some issue, but she had no right to press him if he didn't want to share—especially now, since they were only friends and nothing more.

They *were* friends, right? She glanced back over at Derek. Maybe this entire trip was a way to heal those old scars and finally get that closure she'd been seeking so she could move on with her life. She still wasn't interested in dating anyone, but it was nice to finally close the door on some of the feelings of inadequacy and hurt their relationship had caused. "I think it's time to ask our host to call for help. What do you think?"

"Agreed," Derek said. He stood, then saw Lee out of the corner of his eye working in the kitchen and motioned with a friendly gesture for the man to join them. Lee came over carrying a cup of coffee and settled himself in a brown recliner while Derek and Flynn sat together across from him on the chocolate-colored couch they had been leaning against moments before.

"Y'all feel better after that nap?" Lee asked.

"And the food," Derek added. "Your food was a real lifesaver."

Lee smiled at the compliment. "I used to be a cook at a diner down in Frisco. Nothing fancy, but fast and tasty usually fit the bill."

"Ah! No wonder your food was so good!" Flynn

smiled. "We didn't really get a chance to talk earlier." Her voice was still a bit scratchy from swallowing that lake water, but she cleared her throat and went on. "I want to thank you for allowing us in your home and feeding us so well."

"You're very welcome. Now, y'all want to tell me what you're doing walking around out there and swimming in my lake? I don't get many visitors up here, especially ones that look like they've been lost in the wilderness with a kid in tow." He said it with a smile, but there was both a curiosity and a hard tone to his voice that didn't seem to match his friendly, grandfatherly demeanor up until now. Or maybe she was just now picking up on the nuances of his behavior and speech because she had been so out of sorts after the episode at the lake. Either way, Flynn's radar immediately went up. The situation seemed innocuous enough, but being a cop, she had learned quite a bit about watching body language and listening to people when they talked to gather hints about their veracity. The man seemed stiff and oddly anxious. Something just wasn't right. Maybe Lee just didn't like unannounced visitors? Or was there more to it? Up until now, he'd been the perfect host, but had he just been putting on a show?

Before Flynn could even answer, Derek jumped in. "We had some trouble with our vehicle and ended up walking. It has been a rather harrowing experience, and we'd like to get back to town as soon as we can. Actually, if you have a phone, we can call for help and be on our way. And I insist you let us pay you for the food we ate."

Vehicle? Not helicopter? Still, Flynn bit her tongue and let Derek's comment go. He must have sensed the same red flags that she was seeing with Lee's deportment and was being careful with his language.

Lee shook his head. "No payment is necessary." He sat back a little in his chair. "Unfortunately, I can't let you borrow a phone."

Derek raised his eyebrows, but before he could comment, Lee raised his hands. "I don't have a phone. Can't let you use something I don't have. I'm pretty remote and can't get a landline, and cell service is also almost nonexistent in this neck of the woods, so I just never bothered. I do have a ham radio, though. If you tell me who to call, I can probably get a message out for you."

Derek nodded, but his features were still alert. "That would be great. My assistant's name is Candice O'Rourke. She lives down in Frisco. If you could get a message to her and give her this address, she could send her brother up in his truck to get us. He's got chains and four-wheel drive and can probably make it through. He's also a pretty good mechanic and might even be able to fix our vehicle if it's not too complicated and he has the parts."

"Well, we can give it a try," Lee said with a smile. He gave Derek a notepad and pen, and Derek wrote down the name and phone number. Lee gave Derek a smile, then headed down the hallway.

"Why didn't you tell him about the helicopter and the drug dealers?" Flynn asked.

Derek shrugged. "I don't know. I was getting a strange vibe from him. I just thought caution seemed more prudent. He doesn't need to know our business."

"I agree. I'm not sure what it is, but something is off about the way he's acting now. Maybe we should just start walking again? I feel like we're on borrowed time here. We've already been here longer than I'd hoped. What if he somehow has a connection with the drug dealers?"

"Anything is possible," Derek agreed. "But I'm not sure walking is the best option, either. I'm worried about you."

"I can make it," Flynn said fiercely. "My chest hurts a little, but otherwise I'm good to go. That food and rest did wonders for me."

"What about Kevin?"

Flynn glanced over at the boy, who was still sleeping soundly. "The rest and food have been good for him, too. We can both make it. We'll do whatever it takes."

Derek tilted his head. "I wonder if he really does have a ham radio or if he's been lying this whole time." He ran his hands through his hair. "Do you still have that pistol?"

Flynn frowned. "It should be in my coat pocket. The lake water probably ruined my phone, but I bet that gun will still fire, and the small camera I had in there is waterproof, so it should be fine, too." She stood and went over to where her coat was still hanging on the back of the chair where Kevin had put it. The coat was mostly dry, and the pistol and camera both seemed in good shape. Her phone, as predicted, was waterlogged.

"Guess I'll need a new one of these once we get back into town. I don't think a bucketful of rice would help. The case said it was waterproof, but I bet that didn't mean it could take a dunking in a frozen Colorado lake at these temperatures." She smiled to herself, determined to find the good even in a bad situation. She was alive and hopefully they would be rescued soon. She checked her boot as well and breathed a sigh of relief once she saw that the SD card with the photos from the crime scene was still tucked safely inside the lining. Water wouldn't hurt the card, but she had wondered if it had fallen out and gotten lost when she'd gone in the lake. Thankfully, it was right where she'd left it. She really did have a lot to be thankful for.

"Keep your gun handy," Derek advised. "I'm hoping we won't need it, but anything is possible."

Flynn nodded, her good mood slipping away as these new perils started to weigh down on her shoulders. They weren't saved yet, and they couldn't relax their vigilance until they were sitting in the police station downtown, telling their story to the local law enforcement team. "I think I'll change back into my own clothes while I have a chance." She gathered her things from the around the fireplace and easily found a bathroom down the hall. She could hear voices from behind a closed door but couldn't make out the words. It certainly sounded like Lee was using his ham radio, but had he actually called Candice as he promised he would do?

She returned shortly with the handgun stowed in her waistband and covered by her flannel shirt. Everything was dry except for her coat, which only had a few damp spots. She adjusted the sleeves and moved it closer to the fire, hoping the remaining sections would dry quickly. As soon as she finished, Lee came back into the room.

"Well, that's done," he said mildly.

"Did you have any trouble reaching your friend with the radio?" she asked.

"None at all. He keeps his ham radio on most days and just listens to the chatter. He lives down in Frisco, and he was happy to call Ms. O'Rourke right then while I waited on the radio. He had her on Speaker, and I could hear her talking in the background. She said she'd been really worried about you three, and she'd send someone up to give you a ride down right away. We're a fair distance away from Frisco, though, so it might take some time for them to get here, and the roads are bad due to yesterday's storm. I hope you don't mind waiting a little longer."

Flynn sat back on the couch. "No problem for us, as long as you aren't too terribly inconvenienced. We sure appreciate your help, but I imagine you probably had other plans for the day that didn't include helping out a group of strangers." She leaned back, making sure her shirt covered the bulge from the weapon. Was she right to be wary of this man? He'd done nothing but help so far, but she was still getting an uncomfortable feeling that something wasn't just right. She watched his eyes, which seemed to dart around the room, and he kept playing with the hair at his nape, as if he was uncomfortable and his shirt collar was just a bit too tight.

"I didn't have any real plans beyond reading the latest Lee Child novel. I can always pick that up later." Lee returned to the recliner where he'd previously been sitting and began chitchatting about the storm that had hit the previous day and all the commotion it had caused. "I was listening to the radio most of the day yesterday. That snow and wind caused quite a bit of hardship. I'm really sorry you folks got caught up in it, too." The topic seemed innocuous enough, but Flynn still got the feeling that the older man was on edge and was no longer the kind and benevolent host he had pretended to be.

Suddenly the doorbell rang and sent an alert down

Flynn's spine that interrupted her musings. They had a visitor? Here? Now?

"Hmm. I wonder who that could be," Lee said in a deceptively friendly tone.

Flynn's head snapped toward the front door. They hadn't heard a vehicle, and although she didn't know the area well, it seemed way too soon for anyone from Frisco to have arrived at the cabin, especially based on Lee's own comments that it would take some time for anyone to reach them. As Lee rose to go to the door, Flynn reached over and gave Kevin a little shake. "Kevin? Wake up and get your boots on." She didn't know what to expect, but she did want to be ready if things suddenly went south in a hurry.

The boy stirred and then started slowly putting on his boots. He crinkled his brow but said nothing as he obeyed her request. His eyes met hers, and she tried to telegraph a need for caution without scaring him.

Derek tensed on the couch and turned slightly so he had Lee in his line of vision as the older man went to answer the door. In an abundance of caution, he pulled his weapon but kept his gun hand down and hidden from anyone by the front door. He heard Lee release the lock, and a tingle of adrenaline shot down his arms.

Suddenly, the door crashed open and two young men wearing blue coats and skull caps burst into the living room brandishing pistols. Derek instantly raised his weapon, and his first shot caught the first man through the door in the chest. He went down with a grunt as a circle of red instantly spread around his upper body. The second man reacted quickly. He pulled Lee in front of him, grasping him around the neck and using him as a shield while also pointed a .45 pistol at Lee's head.

Derek had no time for a second shot that wouldn't also endanger their elderly host. He quickly glanced over at Flynn, who had dropped behind the couch on the floor, pushing Kevin with her. He leaned down on the couch himself, trying to make a smaller target of his body.

"Unless you want me to shoot this old man, you'd better put that gun down," the aggressor stated in a deep, nasty tone.

"Unless you want me to shoot you, you should put your gun down," Derek responded in a calm voice, instantly thankful for the military training that had honed his firearm skills. He was an excellent shot, yet he didn't want to put Lee at risk if it wasn't absolutely necessary.

"That's not going to happen," came the dark response.

Derek saw a gleam in the man's eye and thought he recognized the voice as the more mature of the two men who had been chasing them when they had spent the first night in the mountain cave. Nervous men often made mistakes, but this man seemed in complete control and a formidable adversary. He remembered the man's fortitude and commitment to the cause when he and his partner been out searching for them in the bitter cold. If it was the same guy, he would not give up easily, if at all.

Derek adjusted his aim slightly, but despite his skills, there was no way to get off a shot without also putting Lee in danger. Although Derek had some doubts about Lee, he wasn't ready to take a chance on shooting him or getting into a gun battle with Flynn and Kevin so close behind him. His mind raced. "I guess we've reached a draw, because I'm not putting down my weapon. Maybe you should just go back out that door and take your dead friend with you."

The perpetrator gave an evil smile and pushed his pistol into Lee's temple. "I'm not inclined to leave just yet. But I will shoot this guy right here and now if you don't surrender your weapon."

"And as soon as you do, I'm going to shoot you," Derek said, his voice cool.

"And then I'll kill this pretty little lady of yours."

That raspy, deadly voice was new—and totally unexpected.

Derek's head snapped around as he quickly looked back to where Flynn had been crouching only moments before. Two other killers had apparently come in from the back of the cabin and silently approached as he'd been occupied with the drama at the front door. The first man was tall and wearing a red coat. He had dark hair and eyes that seemed cold and unmoving, just like the other perpetrators, and he pointed a 9mm Glock right at Flynn's head. His other arm was around her neck, holding her motionless. A second man in a green coat was holding Kevin tightly against his chest. He had a hand over the kid's mouth, and a gun in his other hand was pointed at Derek. Kevin's eyes rounded, and his face had paled. As Derek watched, the boy started to tremble.

"Your move, friend," the man at the front door said calmly. "What's it going to be?"

Derek's breath seemed frozen in his throat. His kept his gun trained on the man holding Lee, but his eyes darted to Flynn's and held. He saw anger there in those blue depths, but also vulnerability and fear. Would she try to fight her captive's hold? Would he have enough time to save them all? He couldn't lose Flynn. Intrinsically, he knew keeping a cool head was important in dire circumstances like this, but he couldn't stop the fear from invading his heart.

And what if he was wrong about Lee? He probably could only take one shot before one of the three aggressors also fired, killing at least one of the innocent people in the room. Sweat beaded on his forehead, and a knot twisted in his chest.

Could he sacrifice Lee for a chance to save Flynn and Kevin? Was saving both Flynn and Kevin even possible?

THIRTEEN

"I'm going to give you to the count of three to put that gun down, and if you don't, I'm going to shoot this woman." Red Coat pulled her even tighter against him, and Flynn gave an involuntary yelp as the man's rough handling pulled her neck into an unnatural position. The perpetrator's voice was deadly and still calm, as if they were discussing the weather on a hot summer day.

Derek had no doubt he would do exactly what he threatened.

"One."

Derek's hand started shaking imperceptibly, and the weapon suddenly felt heavy and cold in his hand. Would they all die if he surrendered his weapon? Could he live with himself if Flynn was shot dead in front of him and he could have prevented it?

"Two."

"You win," Derek said with resignation in his voice. He pointed his weapon toward the ceiling, making it clear he was no longer a threat, and put his other hand up in mock surrender. There was no time to consider it further. Flynn and Kevin might survive if he waited for a better opportunity to escape. If he tried to fight back now, someone would probably get shot.

Green Coat reached over and took his gun, then secured it in his waistband as he pushed Kevin into the chair where Flynn's coat was drying. At the same time, Red Coat frisked Flynn, found the sidearm and took it away from her. He pocketed it, then forced her to sit in the other chair next to Kevin.

Derek's eyes returned to the front door. The blue-coated man released Lee and pushed him aside, causing the older man to stumble and fall to his knees. The gunman stepped over his fallen colleague, who lay dead on the floor, then turned and shut the front door firmly behind him. With a click, he engaged the dead bolt.

"We don't want to be interrupted, do we?" he said with a smirk.

Lee pulled himself back up to his feet. "You sure took your time getting here," he complained with a nasal tone. "I've been watching over them for hours."

So Lee Clark was the enemy after all. Derek clenched his teeth. The man should get an Oscar for his acting ability. He'd put on quite a show.

"We weren't in a rush once we knew where they were," Blue Coat replied. "Believe it or not, we've actually got a lot going on today. This was high priority, but not as high as making sure our out-of-town guests were properly greeted."

"Harrumph," Lee said acerbically. Right before Derek's eyes, the old man's countenance changed from one of a benevolent grandfatherly type to a look of greed and fury. "You're going to have to pay me more if you want me to babysit for you. I agreed to be a courier, nothing more, and you already don't pay me enough for the risks I take."

Blue Coat turned, raised his weapon and fired at Lee's chest before the man could say another word or even realize the danger he was in. A dark red circle started to slowly spread across his shirt as he gasped and sputtered. "Consider yourself paid."

Lee sank slowly to his knees, then fell forward, his face now registering surprise before his eyes went completely blank. Behind him, Derek could hear Flynn groan as Lee's body hit the floor. Kevin whimpered, but to his credit, he didn't cry out.

Some static sounded from a radio in Blue Coat's pocket, and he pulled out the transmitter and pushed a button. "We're ready for our ride."

The answer was quick in coming. "We're still about five minutes out. We'll be there shortly."

"Ride?" Derek asked, keeping his eye on both the man's eyes and his gun hand.

"Our boss wants to ask you a few questions before he kills you and disposes of your bodies. Don't worry, nobody will ever find them."

"Who's your boss?" Flynn asked.

Blue Coat laughed. "You'll find out soon enough. And really, of all the things you should be worried about right now, his name is definitely at the bottom of the list."

So, they weren't going to kill them right away. That was important news, but the man's tone was so nasty that his words still sent a chill down Derek's spine.

Red Coat pulled some zip ties out of his pocket. "Put on your coats," he ordered all three of them with a sneer.

The three of them stood and put on their coats and gloves, and then Red Coat quickly zip-tied Flynn's and Kevin's hands in front of them. Green Coat started to do the same with Derek, and for a moment, Derek considered trying to fight him off. He glanced around the room, trying to think of any feasible way to escape, and ended up locking eyes with Flynn. She gave an almost imperceptible shake of her head, and the look she gave him made him decide not to chance it—at least not right now. After all, despite whatever orders the man had from the boss, in the blink of an eye, he'd had no trouble at all ending Lee's life. He decided to wait and hope for a better opportunity.

Each of the invaders grabbed one of the captives by the arm and led them around the fallen bodies and out onto the front porch. Years of working as an aviator helped Derek identify the sound of the rotors before the helicopter was even visible, and a short time later, a chopper bearing the logo of Bear Creek Vacation Rentals approached and landed in the snow-covered area between the cabin and the lake.

A sinking feeling settled in Derek's gut. They were planning to kill them for sure. Otherwise, there was no way they'd let them all see the connection between the drugs, murders and Bear Creek. Still, a new resolve also formed. They weren't beaten yet. He prayed for God to give him an opportunity, any opportunity, to help the three of them escape without getting hurt.

The helicopter ride was short, less than half an hour, and Flynn immediately recognized the clearing as they started to land near the place where they had first seen the dead bodies in the field. There was no sign of the murders now, and it appeared that the snowstorm had completely covered up whatever crime-scene cleanup had been accomplished. Smoke rose from the chimney on the large log cabin–style house, but the building still looked rather dilapidated, although it was clear that it was in use. As they landed, they could see several new tarps covering some large, bulky items under the pole barn that hadn't been there before. She didn't have a clue what was under those tarps, but it was interesting that the area that had previously looked abandoned now had so much life teeming around it and had a cleaner and neater appearance overall.

They landed on the helicopter pad near the house in the middle of the field and were met by four new men, who came out of the house garbed in dark heavy winter clothes, as if they were soldiers from a winter clime in some remote country. Each was carrying a high-powered rifle, and they all looked very adept at using them. Were they mercenaries? They sure fit the part. A couple of snowmobiles were parked near the house's front door, and it was obvious that the helicopter pad had been blown and cleaned, as had a path through the snow to the main house and the outbuildings.

"Where do you want them? Inside the cabin?" Red Coat asked the leader of the new group of men as he dragged the captives, none too gently, out of the helicopter one by one onto the concrete pad. He grabbed Kevin's arm and started to walk the boy toward the big main house before he got an answer, but the man in charge of the military-looking group raised his hands and stopped him. "Hold on. There's a meeting going on inside. No one else goes in."

Red Coat shrugged. "Fine. Where to, then?"

Another man approached from the vicinity of the pole

barn, wiping his hands on an oily rag as he walked. He had a scruffy beard and long dark hair that he'd pulled back in a ponytail and was wearing a black skull cap. Flynn noticed his teeth were damaged, as if he was or had been a heavy methamphetamine user. Still, he was large and muscular and had the look of someone who had no problem hurting other people. Once he arrived, the others that had tied them up and guarded them on the helicopter gave him a measure of deference, so Flynn guessed he had some measure of power on the compound.

"They don't need to see any more than they've already seen. The workroom behind the barn will serve just fine. Go ahead and take them over there," the scruffy man responded. He pocketed the rag and put his hands on his hips as he surveyed the captives. Flynn noticed he was wearing dark green snow overalls and heavy black boots, both covered with grime. She wondered if he was some sort of mechanic, or if he had some other role. Even though his appearance was unkempt and that of a mountain man who hadn't seen civilization in a long time, he carried himself as if he was in charge, and the other men definitely gave him respect and looked to him for direction. Even the soldiers seemed to be waiting for his orders.

"Well, you gave us quite the chase," Mountain Man said with a smile as he eyed each of the captives. "I'd love to hear how you survived the night during that storm."

Flynn shrugged. "I'm not a storyteller. You'll have to wait for the movie."

He smiled and raised a gloved hand to roughly grab

her chin, but she pulled away. His smile instantly disappeared, and a hard, flint-eyed expression took its place. "You'll tell me what I want you to tell me. Understand? You don't have a choice."

"It's pretty cold in there," Red Coat said. "You sure you want them in that room?" He never quite looked the newcomer in the eye, and Flynn wasn't sure if he was worried about them freezing—or himself if he was unfortunate enough to pull guard duty. She was glad they'd at least allowed them to put on their coats before taking them from Lee Clark's house.

"It won't matter," the man responded gruffly. "They aren't going to be there that long. We'll have ourselves a conversation, and then you'll be free to dispose of them however the boss wants it done."

Flynn met Derek's eyes and saw frustration and simmering anger. She turned to look at Kevin, hoping to instill new confidence and hope into the boy's sullen expression. He had to be scared. She was scared herself, and probably even Derek was a bit insecure about their current situation—it was obvious he didn't like the mountain man touching her.

But she would not give up. The God they served was a big God. Nothing was impossible, and she refused to give up, just because things were looking pretty bad. The small flame of hope still burned inside her. Somehow, they would find a way out of this mess. They just had to.

Their captors left the militia-looking group behind and pulled them past the pole barn and toward a small shed attached to the back right corner of the structure. Flynn still couldn't tell what was underneath all the tarps, but some of the items looked like big barrels of

chemicals. Were the barrels full of substances and supplies used to cook meth? She didn't know the entire rec-
ipe but wouldn't be surprised if they were stocking up.
Twice, the perps had mentioned visitors and it being a
big day today. Were they trying to woo and impress a
new buyer or supplier? Anything was possible, and she
made mental notes of what she was seeing, just in case
it would help with the prosecution once they got to tell
their story to law enforcement.

Apparently, while their small party had been trying
to escape down the mountain, the people here had been
working hard to clean the place up. The old truck and
other trash had been removed. A large fire pit was behind the pole barn, and sizable hunks of burned wood
and other unidentifiable items were strewn about in the
center and looked like the remains of a bonfire. As the
small group approached, a man on a bulldozer was busy
covering up the pit by pushing dirt and snow over the
contents. There were other implements under the pole
barn that weren't covered, including a snowplow attach-
ment and a large box blade that were probably used for
road repairs. Near the back of the barn, she saw two
faded metal signs that advertised Bear Creek Vacation
Rentals. She also noticed a few more snowmobiles on
the right, and a couple of them looked like they were
being worked on. Tools and rags littered a short workbench and the surrounding area.

When they reached the small room, Red Coat pulled
out a set of keys and unlocked the door, then flipped
up the light switch on the left-hand wall. Two shelving
units covered the back wall and were filled with boxes
of gadgets, dust and outdoor yard supplies. Another wall

had racks of snow supplies, including snowshoes, fishing equipment and skis. In the middle of the room, a long table was surrounded by several wooden chairs. Flynn wasn't sure, but if she had to guess, she could imagine a group of dealers sitting around that table, dividing up packets of meth for distribution. There was a small heater in the corner, but the room was drafty, and even though Blue Coat turned the heater on as soon as he entered the room, it did little to combat the cold that permeated the air and seemed to soak into her bones.

"Tie them to the chairs," Blue Coat ordered. He searched through the boxes on the shelf but only found a couple of rolls of duct tape. "Use this," he ordered, and threw one to Green Coat, who forced them to sit and then started securing them to the chairs. He cut the zip ties with a pocketknife and then taped each arm to the arm of the chair and each ankle to a chair leg. Finally, he taped each captive to the back of the chair as tightly as he could around the chest.

Flynn flexed her muscles and tried to puff out her chest and shoulders, just in case that little bit would help if they were ever given the chance to escape, but she doubted it made any difference. She could barely move.

"They were armed," Green Coat offered once he was done. He put on the table the gun he'd taken from Flynn and also the small camera she'd been carrying and her ruined cell phone. Red Coat followed suit and put the pistol he'd taken from Derek beside it. The navy backpack they'd been using was nowhere around, and Flynn figured it had gotten left behind at Lee Clark's house, along with Derek's phone.

"Okay, go secure the area," Mountain Man ordered.

He pulled back a chair and seated himself as close to the heater as possible, picking up the guns and inspecting them as he did so. He picked up the camera, too, powered it on and then scanned through the photos. Seeing nothing that caught his eye, he flipped it back on the table.

"From those photos, it looks like you're having a great vacation," Mountain Man said in a conversational tone.

"We were until your men shot at us," Flynn replied caustically.

He smiled in response, but it was an evil smile.

"Want me to stay?" Blue Coat asked.

"Yeah, stick around and guard that door, just in case they start thinking escape is even possible." He turned and studied the three captives as the other men filed out, leaving Blue Coat by the door with a rifle someone handed him on their way out. "Escape isn't possible, you know, but I'd sure like for you to try. We could use some excitement to break up the day."

"We didn't give you enough of a thrill by making you spend two days chasing us down the mountain?" Derek replied, his tone derisive.

Mountain Man grinned, his entire countenance changing back to the good ole boy persona, as if he was an old buddy and they were just sitting around talking about the weather. "Well, that was a bit of fun, up until our friend Lee had to go and get greedy. He wanted quite a sum for finding you three, but we decided not to pay his price." He pulled off his gloves and held his hands out toward the heater. "Apparently, you also gave the boys some target practice with your helicopter." He raised an eyebrow. "Iraq?"

Derek looked away, apparently unwilling to give the

man any information about his service to the country
or anything else.

As a law enforcement officer, Flynn was familiar
with a variety of interrogation techniques and wasn't
surprised by Derek's response—or lack of one. His military training had probably been similar to her own, so
he likely knew all the tricks. This man's first attempt
seemed to be feigning friendship, but she wasn't fooled
by his suddenly sociable demeanor, and they'd already
seen his true personality come out once. She glanced at
Kevin, knowing that with him in the mix, it would ultimately be impossible to keep secrets, regardless of what
method Mountain Man used. She would do anything to
protect the boy—anything—and any decent interroga-
tor would know that. Still, if there was any way to drag
this out, it might allow that much more time for planning and executing an escape attempt.

"So let's start with introductions," Mountain Man
said. "You can call me Sam." He glanced at Derek. "According to the registration from the downed whirlybird,
you're Derek King."

"Guilty," Derek said through gritted teeth. "No how
about you let me take these nice people home? They've
already been through more than they bargained for."

"Well, that's not going to happen," Sam said as he
made a clicking sound with his tongue. He motioned
toward Flynn. "This your wife and kid?"

"Nope. I'm not married," Derek replied, his tone now
taking on a bored, disinterested tone. "They're just customers, plain and simple."

Sam narrowed his eyes as if he didn't quite believe
him, then turned to Flynn. "That true?"

Flynn instantly understood Derek's strategy. "Of course. Why would he lie? We hired Mr. King to give us a sightseeing tour. You probably even found my expensive camera by the helicopter. It was too heavy for me to carry, but maybe you can give it back to me now?" She prayed they didn't know anything about photography and hadn't noticed the missing SD card. She rambled on, trying to bolster her story. "I hope the cold weather didn't damage it. I'm visiting from Florida, and the mountains here are beautiful and very different from what I'm used to. Y'all don't have a beach in sight." If she distanced herself from Derek in this man's eyes, hopefully he wouldn't use them as leverage to get Derek to comply with whatever he had planned. She wanted to do the same with Kevin so he also had a chance to survive, but it was harder to explain the child's presence. She hoped she could just avoid describing their relationship, but realized the attempt would probably be futile.

"Really? So, you're telling me you're just a tourist?" Sam leaned over and brushed his hand suggestively over Flynn's cheek. She forced herself not to react but saw Derek tense out of the corner of her eye. She didn't think she was in any real danger of being molested. The man was just trying to get a rise out of her or Derek to test the veracity of their words.

"Why don't you just tell us what you want?" Flynn said quickly, trying to keep the man's attention on herself instead of on Derek. "We don't even know why you shot us down in the first place. Are you and your men in the habit of shooting tourists out of the sky?"

"I don't believe that tourist story for a minute," Sam said as he leaned back, his smile once again disappearing. He furrowed his brow, and his features hardened. "I want to know who you are and why you're up here on this mountain." He locked eyes with Flynn. "And unless I like your answers, I'm going to kill this boy slowly and painfully right here in front of you."

FOURTEEN

Flynn watched Sam carefully. His eyes were dark, and there was a coldness there that had quickly erased any hint of friendliness. She heard Kevin whimper, but she kept her attention on the evil man in front of her. They'd gotten to the threats faster than she'd thought, but obviously, this guy wasn't playing games.

"Okay, fine. The boy has nothing to do with this, and neither does the pilot, so leave them out of it. In fact, you should let them both go right now so the two of us can settle this. I'm the one you want. My name is Flynn Denning, and you or someone in your organization shot my sister a few days ago in Frisco. I'm here to find out why."

Sam digested her words, then nodded. "So, you're that cop's sister."

"That cop has a name. It is Erin. Erin Denning. And she's still in the hospital, fighting for her life, because of you or someone here on your payroll."

He shrugged. "Now we're getting somewhere." He glanced from Derek to Kevin. "But no one is leaving here today, whether they're related to that cop or not."

"Then there's no reason why you shouldn't tell me why Erin was shot. She's my only sibling. Her life matters, and somebody tried to take that away from her. If you're going to kill me anyway, you might as well satisfy my curiosity." She tilted her head. "And I'm very curious." She felt Derek tense again at the challenge in her words but couldn't regret her tone. This man seemed proud of his crimes and his voice and body language were begging for an audience. He wanted others to think he was smart and organized.

The man laughed outright. "You have a point." He ran his fingers over her pistol, which was still in his grip but pointed away from their group, as if he was considering his words. He didn't speak, though, so Flynn prompted him.

"Bear Creek Vacation Rentals is a front, right?" Flynn said, pushing the envelope. She heard Derek make a noise, but didn't back down. "You're just using that company to launder the money you make selling meth up and down the Rockies. Am I right?" She narrowed her eyes. "My sister found out about your business and started investigating, so you had her shot to get her out of the way. You hoped that if you killed her before she got any farther, then the investigation would die with her."

Sam drew his lips into a thin, unrepentant line. "You are remarkably well informed." Suddenly, he stood and motioned to Blue Coat. "Stay here and keep an eye on them. I'll be back." He pocketed the camera and one of the pistols, then handed the other pistol to Blue Coat as he left the room and closed the door firmly behind him. Blue Coat zipped the pistol into his coat pocket, then moved over by the door and took up a sentry pose, his rifle on his back and his arms crossed.

Derek looked over at Flynn and lowered his voice for

her ears only. "Well, you were right. At least now we know why your sister was hurt. I don't even think that they care that we saw the murders, although that's one more strike against us. We know about the drugs, we know they shot Erin and we saw them murder Lee Clark. To their way of thinking, they have to get rid of us."

"Something tells me they're in a hurry to do so, too. What did that one guy say back at Lee's house? That something else big was happening today?"

Blue Coat stood up straighter by the door. "Shut up, the two of you."

They complied, but Flynn's mind was turning. There was no sign of the murdered drug dealers outside, but that wasn't the only change. The buildings and surrounding area had been spiffed up since they'd seen the bodies two days ago. Why were they cleaning up?

She rapidly considered several possibilities but discarded them all. Before she could dig even further, there was a noise at the door, and Blue Coat moved aside as another man came in. He was tall, broad shouldered and wearing a very expensive-looking gray woolen double-breasted suit with a burgundy power tie and a black topcoat. His designer leather shoes had to be custom-made, and his black leather gloves appeared luxurious and sleek, completing the ensemble. Once he entered, he pulled off his gloves and then smoothed down his wind-blown hair with manicured fingers. He was obviously wealthy and very concerned about his appearance, even in this drafty, dilapidated structure out in the middle of the wilderness.

"So, you've destroyed my helicopter." The man's voice was calm, yet almost teasing.

Derek shook his head. "No, *you* destroyed *my* helicopter. I think I'm entitled to a refund. You sold it to me and then had your men shoot me out of the sky. That wasn't part of our deal."

The suited man shrugged as Flynn's eyes flew back and forth between the two men. Suddenly, the pieces clicked together as Flynn listened to the conversation. Adam Cary stood before them—the man who had sold Derek his company. He was also the owner and CEO of Bear Creek Vacation Rentals.

Adam took the empty seat across from the three captives and took a moment to look each one up and down. He was totally unaffected by the fact that they were taped securely to the chairs or that one of the three was indeed a child. Despite his friendly demeanor, under the surface, there was a calculating coldness to his persona, and the air suddenly felt thick and malevolent. "You should have stayed in your lane, Derek," he finally said, turning his attention back to the pilot. "There was no reason to come flying up this high. We picked this location for a reason. I simply can't afford to have you know about us and what we're doing up here. You understand, right?"

"I understand that you're nothing but a drug dealer, dressed up in a fancy suit." Flynn bit out the words. "And you had someone try to kill my sister."

Adam slowly turned his head toward Flynn and appraised her flippantly with his eyes, as if she had no value and was beneath his notice. "Ah yes, Erin Denning. I'm afraid she stuck her nose where it didn't belong."

"So, you tried to murder her? Is that how you treat anyone that crosses you?"

Adam shrugged. "It's the cost of doing business. A few pawns have to be sacrificed for the good of the organization. Collateral damage is unavoidable."

"Lee Clark was a pawn. He was on your team and he got in your way, so your man killed him. But Erin is a detective. She wasn't one of your game pieces that you can just dismiss and take off the board. She plays for the other team. She's going to get better, and then she's going to arrest you and shut you down. This is the beginning of the end for you. I hope you like wearing the color orange, Mr. Cary. I hear it's all the rage in prisons these days."

Adam laughed. "Quite a feisty friend you have here, Derek," he said with a smile.

Cary's reaction made it clear he didn't think much of her threat, but Flynn just couldn't keep her mouth shut. She had finally found the man responsible for trying to kill her sister. Her enemy now had a face and a name. Anger and disgust bubbled inside her, and she wanted nothing more than to slap the handcuffs on his manicured hands and drag him to jail. She pulled at her bonds in frustration, but the tape held fast. "I might not be able to stop you, but my sister will. You've failed. You're going to be sorry you ever set up shop in Colorado."

Adam's face contorted and became a mask of prideful maliciousness right in front of them. He stood and fisted his hands, as if he was about to strike. "No one is going to stop me. I'm the most powerful man in the valley, and I'm about to become the most powerful man in the state—maybe even the whole Southwest region."

"And how do you plan on becoming that?" Flynn sneered.

"I'm about to make a deal with a new distributor, and his network doubles what I already own." He leaned closer, his lip curled. "You think one small-town cop is going to change that? Or the three of you?"

"So how did Erin discover your involvement?" Derek asked, apparently trying to divert Adam's anger from Flynn before he struck her or did something worse.

Cary paused a moment, leaned back and glanced back at Derek. His mask of indifference slowly returned. "She came across my stash house in Frisco—and got some of my dealers to talk more than they should have about my mountain lab and our distribution process. I believe you discovered what I do to people who defy me. You saw their bodies, or what was left of them, after I found out about their treachery." He lifted his chin and brushed a fleck of dirt off his coat. "I don't believe in second chances—for anyone. You've all seen too much, which is a pity. I just came by to tell you that you're going to die today. And then I'm going to sit down, have a good meal, and I'm going to kill your sister, too."

His words made the blood in Flynn's veins turn to ice. Apparently, this man killed anyone he perceived as a threat. She watched him go, and Blue Coat followed him out and closed the door behind them, leaving them alone for the first time since they'd arrived. She could hear the two men talking outside the door but could only make out some of the words.

"…in about an hour or so. Just stay here and watch them, then take them…up in the helicopter…dump their bodies…"

Kevin started crying, and Flynn turned to him. "Don't worry, Kevin. We're going to get out of here, and we're going to save your mom."

"How?" he said through the tears. "That man is a monster! He's the one that hurt my mom, and he said he's going to kill her." He swallowed hard, obviously trying to gain control of his rolling emotions. "How can we stop him?"

"Pray," Derek said softly. "We all need to start by praying." He bowed his head. "Lord, we are stuck, and this situation looks really scary, but You are a big God, and nothing is too hard for You. Please show us a way out of this mess and make us strong so we can do whatever it takes to escape and save Kevin's mom. Amen." He leaned forward and kept his voice low. "Okay, in the army, we actually used to play around with how to get free from duct tape, and it's not as hard as it looks." He gave Kevin a wink to bolster his confidence. "So here goes. Just watch what I do. You're actually re-creating the angle where duct tape normally tears. Step one—bring your arms in as hard and fast as you can, as if you're trying to hit yourself in the chest. Got it? Ready? Go!"

Both Flynn and Kevin looked at him dubiously, but he demonstrated, and in one quick motion, the tape tore as he pulled hard against the bonds around his arms. They glanced at each other, then shrugged and copied Derek's actions. A few moments later, they successfully freed their arms as well.

Even though his hands were free, Derek's chest was still taped to the back of the chair. "Okay, now we move to step two. We could try to use our hands to pull off all this tape, but that takes too long. Instead, you have to lean forward really quickly, as if you're going to throw up on the floor between your legs. Ready? Go!" He demonstrated again, and the duct tape that held his chest tore with a satisfying rip. He quickly pulled the tape away, then reached down and freed his feet.

Flynn followed Derek's example and was also able to get her chest free, but Kevin didn't manage it since he was so upset and didn't quite understand how to make the tape tear. Flynn quickly freed her legs and then reached over, freed Kevin and pulled him into a giant bear hug. Derek hid behind the door, waiting for Blue Coat to come back in.

He didn't have to wait long. Blue Coat opened the door only a few minutes later, and his face immediately mirrored his surprise when he noticed the prisoners were all free. He tried to shout, but Derek was quick to pull him into the room, shut the door firmly before anyone could be alerted to what was happening and grab his rifle from him at the same time.

Blue Coat started to fumble with his pocket but wasn't able to pull out anything before Derek gave him a quick punch to the cheek, which sent him reeling backward against the table, unconscious. Flynn grabbed Blue Coat and moved his body to the floor, and once he was down, Derek handed her the man's rifle, then bent down and frisked him and found his pistol in the man's coat. He took the handgun and secured it in his own jacket pocket but didn't find anything else of value. Then he motioned to Kevin. He wanted to make sure the boy had a role in their escape, and this was the perfect way to include him.

"Help me duct-tape him, okay, Kevin?" Derek said

softly. The boy nodded and brought him the remains of the roll of tape, and with Kevin's help, the two secured the man so he couldn't stop their escape.

"Won't he be able to escape like we just did?" Flynn asked as she guarded the door.

"No, we had the advantage of having our hands in front of us, and the angle of the chairs where we were sitting made it easy to tear the tape. This guy is going to be taped with his hands behind him and with his mouth covered. We'll also leave him on the floor. He'll be trussed up just like a Christmas turkey and won't be able to get free—at least not right away. He might eventually manage to escape, but hopefully by that time we'll already be down the mountain."

Derek finished taping up their captor, then leaned Blue Coat's body against the back wall so he was out of the way. Then he joined Flynn, who had swung the rifle onto her back and was quickly going through the boxes on the shelves. "Find anything interesting?"

"Not so far," she replied as she pulled out yet another box and examined the contents. "No weapons or anything else that would help us get out of here." She put that box back and pulled out another. "I don't even really know what I'm looking for. Just something—anything—that will help." She closed up another box and slid it back on the shelf. "I wish we had a way to communicate with the folks down in Frisco so we could warn them and get them to put a guard on Erin before the cartel gets someone down there."

Derek ran his hand through his hair. "Yeah, me, too. I guess the only thing we can hope for is that Adam was telling us the truth—he wants to kill Erin himself, and he's in no hurry to go to Frisco and commit the crime. If that's the case, we might have a fighting chance of beating him to the hospital."

"How?" Kevin asked with renewed hope in his voice. "How can we beat him?"

FIFTEEN

Flynn felt in her boot, once again verifying that the SD card with the photos of the murdered victims was still safely hidden away. She had seen with her own eyes how the crime scenes had been cleaned up, and by now, any evidence of those heinous acts was probably tainted or destroyed completely. Lee Clark's house had probably also been sanitized, with no evidence of murder left behind. Adam Cary was obviously a very wealthy and powerful man. Flynn was sure he would be a difficult adversary in any venue, but especially in court, where he could afford to hire the best and brightest legal minds to defend him. The photos might not even be enough to do the job of convicting him, but hopefully, with the photos and their own eyewitness testimony, it would be enough. Regardless, they had to try. With renewed energy, she vowed not only to survive and save her sister, but to also see Cary punished for selling poison throughout the state of Colorado.

Unfortunately, they were still stuck in a very remote area, once again without transportation, and in a very snowy and frigidly cold environment. They'd already spent two days trying to get down the mountain and were now back where they'd started, and this time they had no food and were already exhausted from the past two days' exertion. How could they ever make it to the hospital in time to save Erin? "Well, we don't have time to walk down this mountain, and flying seems out of the question. Maybe we can find a car or truck out there somewhere?" She met Derek's eyes. "Do you have any idea how to hot-wire one if we can find one?"

Derek blew out a breath and shrugged his shoulders. "Maybe. If it's an older model. These newer cars and trucks are really hard to start without keys. Most modern cars have ignition immobilizers that make hot-wiring them almost impossible."

"I'm not even sure I saw any cars or trucks out there anyway. It seems like most of them fly in and out…" She snapped her fingers as an idea hit her. "Or use the snowmobiles."

Derek smiled, obviously following her line of thought. "Now those, I might actually be able to hot-wire. They're not nearly as complicated as the new cars out on the road." He moved over to the shelves again and quickly sifted through the boxes, this time pulling out some small hand tools and wires and pocketing them.

"I saw a lot of tarps covering something under the pole barn. Maybe we should start by looking there." She glanced around. "I don't see any cameras in here. Hopefully, there aren't any covering the pole barn, either. Even if there aren't any, though, we need to stay out of sight and hurry to beat Cary to the hospital."

"Agreed," Derek said with a nod. "Even if there aren't any cameras, motion will usually catch someone's eye if they happen to be looking in our direction, so stay down and move slowly so we don't attract attention."

"Sounds like a plan," Flynn said softly. She could tell Derek's words were mostly for Kevin, and she really liked how Derek was including him as an important member of the group. She turned to her nephew, who had calmed down considerably and actually had a look of hope in his eyes. "You can do this, okay? We're going to do everything we can to escape and get down this mountain so we can save your mom. Are you ready?"

He put on a fierce expression. "I'm ready, Aunt Flynn."

"Great! Let's do this!" She spoke quietly but with encouragement and got a nod from the boy in return.

They quietly sneaked out the door, staying low and quiet as they went from tarp to tarp, surreptitiously lifting them up and checking underneath them for a snowmobile or other way to get down the mountain. The first few tarps covered barrels of chemicals, presumably the ingredients needed for manufacturing the methamphetamines in the main cabin. They were labeled, and Flynn made mental notes of the chemicals so she could include them in her report to law enforcement. Two other tarps covered split wood for the fireplace, and they passed two snowmobiles that looked like they were being worked on. The hoods were off both, and tools were strewn around the small workbench. They passed them both, but then hit pay dirt under a musty-smelling gray tarp near the back right corner of the barn. Two snowmobiles, one a red 2015 Yamaha Viper and the other an older 1997 blue Polaris Wedge snowmobile, were both clean and complete and seemed ready to go.

"I hope these are here because they're in working order," she said softly. "Let's hope Sam did a great job repairing them and they'll take us down the mountain without any hiccups."

Derek nodded as he did a quick inspection. They both looked like they were ridden regularly, but looks could be deceiving. Flynn said a quick prayer that they were both still functional.

Derek took off the cover of the red Yamaha and un-screwed the ignition button. Underneath there was a small white square with two large wires coming out. He hit the power switch and let out a sigh of relief as the lights came on, showing that the machine was indeed getting power. Then he pulled out a small length of wire about the size of a large paper clip and bent it into a U. Carefully, he put it in the small white box and touched it to the wire. The engine sputtered but then sprang to life.

He smiled to himself, then motioned for Flynn and Kevin to get on. Flynn slung the rifle onto her back and took the front of the seat, and Kevin quickly got on be-hind her, both with anxious faces but ready to go. Flynn made herself familiar with the dials and gauges on the snowmobile, then continually surveyed the surrounding area, making sure none of Cary's men were approaching.

Derek turned to the Polaris and did a quick inspec-tion of the machine, then raised the hood. "Where is that key switch…" he muttered under his breath. "Ah, here it is." He unplugged it, then pulled the cord, and the motor sprang to life. He quickly moved the tarp out of the way and jumped on the seat, then revved the motor with his gloved hand. "Let's get out of here!"

Suddenly, they heard a shot, and the wood behind Derek's head splintered. Another shot quickly followed.

They quickly sped out from under the barn and headed south, away from the buildings and the shooters. Derek could just hear shouting above the noise of his engine, but he ignored it and focused on staying low on the machine and getting out of there as quickly but safely as possible. His front right ski hit some ice and puddled water, but he shifted his weight, turned with the skid and managed to stay in complete control of the powerful machine.

They moved quickly through the clearing and around the helicopter pad, passing through the area where they'd first discovered the murder victims. Flynn was doing a great job of keeping up—instead of following him, she was driving just slightly back and to his left. That was smart of her, Derek acknowledged. Neither one of them had the proper headgear or goggles to keep the snow out of their faces, and by staying to his side, she avoided the snow spray and water that was flying up behind his snowmobile. He squinted and leaned lower, trying to use the small windshield to block some of the wind that was slapping him in the face. Thankfully, it wasn't snowing right now. The air was cold, but at least it wasn't also wet.

He chanced a look behind him and saw three snowmobiles beginning to pursue them. A few seconds later, he checked again and saw that two of them were still there, but the third had peeled off and was trying to take a shortcut through the trees to cut them off.

They went over a large bump, and Derek once again glanced over at Flynn and Kevin to see how she was managing to drive the unfamiliar machine. So far, they were both handling everything well, and a measure of relief swept over him. Kevin's small body had flown a few inches off the seat as they'd gone airborne for a second or two, but he still had a good grasp on Flynn's waist as they continued down the mountainside, and Flynn wore a look of grim determination that made him proud of her efforts as she piloted the machine.

A sudden realization made him gasp.

He was still in love her.

It hit him with such ferocity that he almost faltered driving his own snowmobile. He gave himself a mental shake and tried to stay focused, yet he couldn't stop the wave of warmth that swept over him as his admission took root. He loved Flynn Denning. Here. Now. He wanted to marry her and spend the rest of his life in her arms. He just had to survive long enough to tell her.

The white snowmobile pursuing them that had separated from the others suddenly broke through the trees and came up on Derek's left. Within moments, it came directly even with Derek's machine, and the driver was pushing it so close that the skis bumped. Derek kicked out at the pursuer two times, then a third, but the driver veered to avoid the blows, and he didn't manage to make contact. A group of trees was not too far ahead of them, and Derek was afraid he would be forced into the trees if he couldn't get the man to back off. Their skis bumped again, and he shifted and pushed at the driver with his hand, trying to force him to turn. The man fought back, and Derek's machine actually went up on one ski as he tried to avoid the pursuer's snowmobile and stay safely away from him, but the man's onslaught didn't stop and he rammed Derek's ride with even more viciousness.

Derek kicked out again and managed to hit the man this time, but still the man attacked, using his own snowmobile to ram Derek's. Derek grimaced at the copse of trees, only yards away now, and pulled hard on the handlebars, hoping he could avoid them at the very last minute without destroying his machine. He leaned low, then put everything he had into one final kick. His boot hit the other man's snowmobile near the front of the hood, and this time it was strong enough that the machine veered left and drove straight into the trees. The perpetrator saw his mistake but couldn't correct his trajectory fast enough, and his snowmobile plowed into the edge of tree line. A branch knocked the driver to the ground, while the snowmobile kept going forward for several yards before crashing into a different tree. Smoke immediately emitted from the hood of the damaged snowmobile, and a loud blast ensued. Derek chanced a look behind him and saw the man moving, albeit slowly, to a crouching position. He was glad he wasn't dead. He wasn't trying to kill anyone. He just wanted to get Flynn and Kevin to safety and save Erin's life too.

One down, two to go.

Derek's face felt like it was freezing, and ice particles were forming on his beard. He slowed enough to bring up his free hand to blow some warm breath on his face, then continued his trek with Flynn and Kevin close behind him. The other two snowmobiles were still back there, too, and gaining fast. Derek considered motioning for Flynn to split up, but he couldn't take a chance that they would follow her and not him, and he desperately wanted to protect her to the best of his ability.

One of their pursuers had a faster, more powerful snowmobile, and after a few more minutes, he was able to pull up alongside Flynn. He bumped her machine, and she cried out but kept control. Derek pulled up alongside him and bumped him from the other side, sandwiching the attacker between them. The trees whizzed by as their speed increased, and Derek leaned closer to the engine, then kicked out as their pursuer bumped Flynn again. Derek met Flynn's eye, and she motioned with her head. He wasn't sure he understood her message, but he hoped he did. She suddenly slowed her snowmobile considerably, and Derek and the drug dealer shot forward, leaving her behind. With one final kick, Derek reached out and made contact, and the other man's snowmobile veered hard to the right and ran right into the trunk of a large tree. An explosion ensued, and flames shot to the sky. The driver lay prone on the ground, away from the explosion but definitely down.

Flynn sped around the disaster and came up next to Derek again. The wind whipped at her hair and skin, but Derek was able to see a look of grim satisfaction on her face as they continued.

Only one pursuer left. This one was apparently not as well versed at driving the snowmobile, but he did start curving to the right in an effort to cut them off as they crested a hill. He probably could have matched or exceeded their speed, but he didn't try. Instead, he suddenly slowed, pulled out a pistol, aimed and fired a shot. The bullet went high, but the loud report shocked both Derek and Flynn, and they flinched at the sound and veered, trying to make harder targets of themselves.

Derek watched helplessly as the man slowed, then steadied himself and once again aimed his pistol at Flynn and Kevin...

SIXTEEN

With a swift flick of his wrist, Derek slowed his ride just enough, then fell back and jolted up beside Flynn and Kevin, effectively blocking them from the shooter's view and using his own body as a shield. The bullet sounded, and with a wave of relief, Derek heard and saw the side of his snowmobile's hood take the hit. The engine sputtered and died, but still he flinched, surprised but exhilarated that the bullet hadn't hit his body. He'd been prepared to give his life for theirs, but it appeared that God had other plans. His snowmobile went forward a few more feet, then stopped once the momentum had given way, leaving a dark trail of engine oil behind him in the snow. Derek quickly jumped off, using the snowmobile as a shield, and pulled out his own pistol. Although Flynn and Kevin were safe, at least for the moment, the man was still coming straight for them and was steadying himself for yet another round.

The shooter didn't get a chance.

Derek's first bullet caught him high in the shoulder, and the man lost his grip and the gun went flying. Derek's second shot rang out in quick procession, and a circle of red instantly began to spread across the man's chest as his snowmobile slowed, then stopped completely. The engine continued running, much like a lawn mower, but the driver slumped over, dead.

Derek pocketed his pistol, said a quick prayer of thanks, counted his remaining bullets and then stood and started walking over to the dead man's machine. He reached it at the same time that Flynn circled back and drove up next to him. She left the motor running, jumped off her snowmobile and flung herself into Derek's arms. Her inhibitions that he'd witnessed up until now seemed to have dissipated, and for several minutes, they just stayed like that, holding each other. He grasped her tightly, so thankful that she was still alive. Death had been knocking at her door, but he hadn't lost her. He reveled in her strength, which buoyed his own. For the first time since Jax's death in the Middle East, he felt whole and hopeful about the future. In fact, the love that pulsed through him was so overwhelming that he had no words, and he felt like he could hold her like this for hours, just relishing her closeness. He bent and kissed her, gently at first, then fuller when her hesitance started to wane and she actually kissed him back.

Finally, the kiss broke. "I can't believe you did that," Flynn exclaimed, her cheeks flushed. "You put yourself right in the line of fire! You saved our lives—again." She reached up, and her gloved hand cupped his bearded chin, brushing away some of the ice and snow that had accumulated there as they'd driven across the snowy tundra. Their breath mingled in puffs of moist air in the cold, crisp weather. "Thank you!"

Before she spoke, he wasn't even sure that she had seen or understood what he had done, but her tone was fierce as she locked eyes with him. She knew. He saw admiration, thankfulness and a whole host of other emotions there that he was afraid to name or even speculate about. Could she still have any feelings at all for him? A part of him wanted to hope—that maybe, just maybe, she did, and if they ever survived this mess, they could fan that flame into a conflagration. She had kissed him back, hadn't she? She had been hesitant at first, but then fire had erupted between them. But what if he was wrong? What if she was just grateful for his sacrifice?

Or what if he was right?

He hadn't dared hope, but if a relationship was a possibility, was he ready for that? He was suddenly swamped with feelings and emotions that surprised him, and even though they were uncomfortable at first, he felt alive and vibrant for the first time in years. She motioned to Kevin to join them, and a moment later, all three of them were huddled together, hugging each other like a tight little family. It didn't bother Derek one little bit. In fact, he gloried in the contact. He pushed all other thoughts aside, including his worry, hope and speculation about the future. For now, he just enjoyed the moment. They were all still alive, and they had a mode of transportation to help get them down the mountain.

Okay, well, he couldn't *completely* push all the other feelings aside. "I would do anything for you," he whispered for her ears alone. "I hope you know that."

She smiled at him. Her eyes were luminous. Was that love shining back at him in those blue depths?

Her expression melted his heart and removed another brick of the prison he had made for himself after Jax's death.

He finally broke the hug, then moved over to the man he had shot. He took off his glove, then reached the man's neck and verified that he was indeed dead. There was no pulse. He pulled his body off the still running snowmobile and laid him under a nearby tree. There wasn't time to bury him. They were still in a race to save Erin, and any moment their adversary could appear and start shooting at them. They had to get back to civilization as soon as possible.

He checked the newly acquired snowmobile's gas gauge and was pleasantly surprised to see that the machine had nearly a full tank and was slightly larger than the model he had been driving. Getting shot at and having to kill a man were horrible ways to acquire a new machine, but at least with the upgrade, they had a fighting chance of making it down the mountain, as long as they didn't encounter any other obstacles.

Just as the thought entered his mind, he heard the familiar sound of rotor blades in the background. As he turned and watched, the Bear Creek helicopter rose ominously above the skyline.

It was headed straight for them.

They weren't safe yet after all.

Flynn heard the noise but didn't recognize it as quickly as Derek. She watched his head snap toward the sound and then saw the worry reflected in his face as the helicopter appeared. It wasn't a military-grade helicopter armed with rocket launchers, but she could easily make out the shapes of two gunmen, one on each side, who each held a high-powered rifle in his hands.

She motioned for Kevin to join her and jumped back

on her snowmobile. Kevin scrambled aboard, and they followed Derek, who had commandeered the dead man's machine and was waving for her to head toward the trees. The forest would slow them down, but it would also slow down the helicopter and give them some much-needed cover. Fear and adrenaline pumped through her veins as she pushed the snowmobile's engine as fast as it could go toward the safety zone.

She made it to the tree line, then followed Derek as he made a hard left down and around a group of aspens. The snowmobile sank quite a bit in the powdery snow but finally gained purchase and surged forward. She felt Kevin shift behind her, but to his credit, he managed to stay on with a tight grip on her waist. She was suddenly grateful for the times she had driven a motorcycle back in college. It had only been a small Honda 250, but it had been quite a lot of fun and gave her at least a basic idea of how to drive the snow machine. Thankfully, she didn't need to shift gears, but the throttle and brakes worked much like her old Honda, and if they didn't have gunmen chasing them and taking shots at them through the canopy of leaves and needles, she would probably be really enjoying the ride.

They continued down through the trees. At one point, Derek had to get off his machine and walk beside it, still directing the big snowmobile by using the grips, throttle and brakes as he pushed it through the deep, powdery mounds of snow. The motor strained and protested, but his actions left a clear path for her to follow. Snow and ice stuck to his black cargo pants and covered him from the chest down, but he got back on the snowmobile and continued, occasionally looking up as he went, making sure that the trees were still providing the cover they needed from the gunmen in the helicopter. He slowed their speed and ducked under branches, and she followed suit, using her legs as well to steady her own Yamaha as it struggled through the snow. Finally, they made it through the thicker areas, and with a little more gas, they were finally able to reach an area where the snow wasn't quite as deep.

They were able to pick up the speed a little but still were forced to stay under the trees. The helicopter's rotors sounded relentlessly above them. They crested a hill, and Derek's snowmobile suddenly went airborne for a few seconds as he drove over a small ledge. He landed without incident and continued, but Flynn took some extra time to go around the ledge instead of over it. Kevin was doing a good job of holding on, but she didn't want to take any more chances than she had to. She caught up to Derek again but continued to drive several feet behind him to stay out of the snow cloud he was kicking up. Her cheeks and lips already felt frozen, and she didn't want to get plastered with any more of the ice or powder that were filling the air. At one point, his snowmobile went up another mound, and he released it so it wouldn't fall backward on him, but it continued running and landed at a good angle, and he jumped back on and bolted forward.

A shot rang out and Flynn recoiled, but neither she, Kevin nor Derek were hit. The gunmen fired some more, but the shots seemed random, meant to scare them since they were well hidden from the helicopter. They could still hear the rotors and got glimpses of the helicopter through the tree branches, but Flynn doubted they could be seen, even through binoculars, in their current location.

Derek slowed as they entered another section of the woods that had a lot of underbrush, and he stood on the running boards, trying to get a better view of where he was going as he drove.

Another shot rang out, but this time, it hit a tree only a few feet away from Flynn, and she cried out involuntarily as the wood splintered in a cloud. Apparently, they were no longer as hidden as they had been only a few minutes before. Were they going to escape from this newest threat? Her muscles tightened as her eyes met Derek's. Then she cried out as the next shot hit Derek with such force that it threw him off his snowmobile and into a large mound of snow.

SEVENTEEN

"No!" Flynn cried out as anguish filled her. "Derek!" She stopped her snowmobile and left it running under some trees but jumped off and rushed over to Derek's side. Another shot rang out that hit an aspen near them, and she screamed in frustration. She couldn't lose him now. There was a look of anguish on his face, and he was breathing hard, but he was still alive. He was lying in the snow, caked with the powder. But now, a bright red splash of blood covered his left shoulder. Hundreds of memories, fears and thoughts flitted through Flynn's mind as she considered the ramifications of his wound.

She couldn't play the what-if game. She had to move Derek, now, and do what she could to save his life. "Can you help me get you out of the line of fire?" she said tightly as Kevin appeared by her right arm, his expression also one of worry and fear. "I don't think I can lift you by myself."

"I'll try," Derek said as he held his left arm as tightly as possible against his body. He'd obviously lost the ability to do much with that arm and was trying to immobilize it the best he could to ease the pain that had to be racing clear to his fingertips. He was such a big man that

Flynn was sure they wouldn't have been able to move him if he hadn't helped, but between the three of them, they were able to get him back behind the trees. A large outcrop of rocks about the size of a set of bunk beds also provided some additional cover, and they huddled behind it, trying to keep the rocks between them and the gunmen. Flynn and Kevin moved Derek as carefully as possible until he was propped up in a sitting position against the rocks. She pulled off the rifle she had been carrying and handed it to Kevin, then she gently peeled back Derek's jacket to look at the wound, hoping that she was also staying beyond the snipers' line of sight.

"It's a serious injury—they must be using a .223 rifle," she muttered under her breath. He cried out as she moved him a little to see his back, and she winced in response. "I'm so sorry! I don't mean to hurt you, but I have to see what we're dealing with." She pulled back the coat a bit more, being as mindful as possible of her movements and how they were affecting Derek's pain level. "Looks like the bullet went straight through." She pulled off her jacket and gloves, removed her flannel shirt, and then put her coat back on before pulling tightly on the fabric so she could rip it into pieces to help stop the bleeding.

Derek shook his head. When he spoke his voice was raspy and laced with pain. "Stop. You need that shirt to keep warm."

"And you need it to live. I'll be okay."

Derek swallowed hard, evidently trying to keep the agony under control. "Okay, but first, take my pistol."

She felt his coat pocket, unzipped it and pulled out the gun.

"Are you a good shot?" he asked. "We only have a few bullets left."

She smiled, hoping to reassure him.

"I ranked sharpshooter the last time I qualified."

"That'll do." Derek nodded. "Use the rifle if you can, but if you run out of bullets, use the pistol. Aim at the helicopter when it gets close enough, and fire at the tail rotor. That will knock them out of the sky. Then we need to get out of here as fast as we can in case any of them survive the landing."

The rotors of the helicopter sounded even louder, and suddenly more shots hit the rocks and ricocheted away from them, while another barrage decimated the tree branches near their hiding place. Then another bullet hit the snowmobile that Flynn and Kevin had been riding moments before. The engine stopped, and suddenly the pungent smell of gasoline filled the air. A moment later, flames shot out of the sides behind the hood, and with a loud crack, the entire machine exploded. A wave of heat hit the three of them, despite the rocks, and knocked both Flynn and Kevin off their feet and into the snow. Bits of engine and other parts flew through the air and landed in all directions, some still on fire as they flew through the sky.

"Flynn! Kevin!"

Derek's voice rang out, but Flynn barely heard it over the roaring in her ears. Still, somewhere in her brain, it registered that they had just lost one of their rides, and they desperately needed to secure the other one if they were going to beat Cary in this race down the mountain to save her sister. She pulled herself up to a sitting position, trying to get her bearings. Kevin moved slightly at her side, and she touched his arm, then met his eyes to make sure he was okay. He nodded at her wordlessly, then started crawling over to Derek's side. Once she knew he was safe, she grabbed the gun she had dropped, as well as the rifle Kevin had been holding, and pulled herself up to her feet and leaned heavily on a tree. There was a bit of dizziness, but it gradually subsided, and sounds from the helicopter seemed to drown out everything else in her head.

She had to stop that helicopter.

She steeled her spine and, using the trees for cover, moved away from the rocks so she could get a clear shot. The shooters noticed she had moved, and moments later, the helicopter was clearly visible as it followed her. It was a fair distance away from her, but she said a silent prayer, hoping that the bird was still within the range of her rifle and her shooting skills hadn't been adversely affected by the explosion and the ringing in her ears.

Dear God, please let my bullets hit the right spot.

She closed her eyes for a moment as she held the weapon, gathering her strength. Then she quickly peeked around the tree trunk, raised the rifle and fired three quick shots at the tail rotor. Answering fire forced her back behind the tree again as her bullets hit metal, but then she heard sputtering noises from the helicopter, and it jerked and tilted strangely, then started spinning in midair. A minute or two later, the helicopter smashed into a stand of trees, and another loud explosion sounded as the entire machine burst into flames. Fire licked at the larger pieces of metal, and a heavy cloud of black smoke filled the air above the crash site.

Thank You, Lord.

She couldn't imagine anyone had lived after that conflagration, but she didn't stick around to find out. Her head was still pounding, but she was gaining more control over the dizziness. She made her way back over to the outcrop of rocks where Kevin and Derek were huddled together.

"Did you get them, Aunt Flynn?"

"I did," Flynn confirmed as she handed him the rifle. "They won't be bothering us anymore, but they could be sending reinforcements. We need to move on as soon as we can. Can you hold on to this?"

Kevin took the rifle again, his expression solemn yet determined. "Yes, I can. Mom taught me how to be careful around guns."

"Excellent," she replied with a nod. She could still hear the faint puttering of Derek's snowmobile in the background, along with crackling sounds from the fire at the helicopter's crash site. She was thankful that her hearing was returning to normal, albeit slowly.

She stored Derek's pistol in her own coat pocket, then picked up her shirt that she had dropped earlier and tore it into several strips. Her rush of adrenaline made her stronger than normal, and the fabric tore easily under her fingers. When she was finished, she balled up two sections of cloth and put them on the entrance and exit wounds, using the folds as makeshift bandages. Then she wrapped more strips as tightly as she dared around his torso and neck so the bandages would be held in place and the bleeding would slow. Finally, she used the last of the fabric to create a sling of sorts to hold his left arm. She could feel the cold starting to penetrate her coat, since she only had on a T-shirt underneath, but the sacrifice was worth it. Derek had saved her life over and over again during the last few days. Bandaging him up after he had taken a bullet on her behalf was the least she could do.

She leaned back on her heels and remembered the words he had spoken softly in her ear, right after he had used his own body to protect her and her nephew from the gunmen. *I would do anything for you…*

What did that mean, exactly?

Did he have feelings for her again? Were they growing inside him like they were in her? She had to admit, she was falling in love with him all over again, and that kiss they'd shared had been something special. She hadn't been looking for love. In fact, she had been dead set against it, ready to push it away with both hands if someone even tried to offer her their heart.

But this was Derek. She had never really stopped loving him. Sure, she had moved on with her life after he had joined the military and left her behind, but if she was being completely honest, she had to admit that her feelings were still very much engaged—especially now, when he was doing everything in his power to keep her and Kevin alive. Would her feelings change when they were back in civilization and Bear Creek Vacation Rentals was closed down for good? Would his? Would he walk away once life returned to normal? Would he break her heart all over again?

She didn't know the answer to that and was almost afraid to speculate. Hope could be a dangerous thing… and could end up crushing her if she misinterpreted his angst and protectiveness during a moment of danger as true love. A large part of her was truly tempted to throw herself into his arms and declare her love, but she would not. If this relationship had any hope of surviving once they got back to Frisco, then Derek would have to make the first move. He would have to share his feelings first.

Enough guessing.

They needed to move. She stopped ruminating, and she and Kevin helped Derek get to his feet then head back over to his snowmobile. She pulled it back from the tree trunk where it had gently landed, then pointed it where they needed to go and got on board. Derek got behind her, and Kevin sandwiched himself in between them, being extra careful not to jostle Derek's arm as he did so, securing the rifle across his lap.

Flynn was worried about how the bumps they were sure to hit would affect Derek's injuries, but they had no choice at all. They had to get down the mountain, and the snowmobile was the only mode of transportation available if they wanted to get to the hospital before Adam Cary. Still, she resolved to drive a bit slower than they had been moving before and be extra careful about both of her passengers. She pulled on her gloves, then revved the engine and started back into the snow, her heart hopeful for the first time in days.

Derek gripped the seat the best he could with his knees, his one good arm still holding tightly to Flynn as she drove. The pain in his shoulder was still very intense, and he was a bit lightheaded from losing so much blood. He let his mind wander as Flynn drove, trying not to focus on his injury, but instead on the job ahead of them. Had Adam Cary already reached the hospital ahead of them? Was Erin Denning already dead? He thought of Kevin, who was snugly between them and probably warmer than he had been since their original crash. The boy already didn't have a father in his life. How would he survive the lost of his one remaining parent? He was just entering the formative years, when he really needed the guidance and help of a father figure in his life.

If Erin was dead, Flynn would need support, too. Yet she didn't even live in Colorado. How could he help her if she returned home right away? He pulled her a tad closer with his good arm and felt a wave of elation sweep over him, despite the circumstances. He had missed her more than he had realized, and now that she was back and he had finally acknowledged his true feelings, he couldn't imagine going back to the empty days he'd trudged through before she had walked out on that tarmac to his helicopter. The fierceness of his protective emotions surprised him, but he didn't dismiss them. Whether Erin was okay or not, he wanted Flynn in his life, and somehow, he was determined to make that happen once this horrible situation with Bear Creek was resolved. He didn't know what that looked like. They lived in different states and had gone down totally different paths. But that was okay. He didn't have to have all the answers right now. He was in love, and everything else was just details that could be figured out once Cary was behind bars.

They drove for a steady half an hour, sticking mostly to the tree line as best they could, just in case an adversary once again appeared. Eventually, they came out of the woods and saw a road up ahead. Pure jubilation soared through Flynn, and was so pronounced that Derek could actually feel it radiate from her, despite the cold. They didn't see any traffic on the road, but it had been recently plowed and the snow was packed and allowed for higher speeds than they'd been able to maintain before. Derek used his good hand to point in the direction they needed to go, and Flynn turned, following his lead. They continued on for several more minutes and finally reached the outskirts of town and some slow, lumbering traffic. They didn't have time to wait, and Flynn sped around the cars on the roadside when necessary, almost as if she was driving a motorcycle around them. Thankfully, the storm from the day before had dumped a heap of snow on the roads and shoulders and made maneuvering relatively easy. A few minutes later, the hospital was in sight. It was a three-story, southwestern-style building with large wooden beams that formed an impressive covered doorway and lobby for the main building, with an emergency room entrance on the side.

Flynn pulled up toward the side of the building, just as Derek noticed a large SUV that was parked near the covered entrance. His heart immediately sank. On the door was a large advertisement for Bear Creek Vacation Rentals, with a huge logo and phone number.

And he could just make out Adam Cary entering the building through the main hospital doors. He felt Flynn stiffen and was pretty sure she had seen both the vehicle and Cary as well. Somehow, they had to stop that man before he could wreak any more havoc on the Denning family.

EIGHTEEN

Flynn jumped off the snowmobile and motioned to Kevin as she pulled off her gloves. "Stay with Derek," she ordered.

"Hold on…" Derek protested as he dismounted. He was a bit awkward with his motion since his arm was still in the makeshift sling, so she helped him briefly, then stepped back.

"I don't have time to argue with you," she responded forcefully. "I need to know that both of you are safe while I do this, and you need to go to the emergency room for that gunshot wound."

Kevin slowly got off the machine, his eyes darting back and forth between the two adults. He was still holding the rifle. "Do you want this?" he asked, his eyes big.

Flynn shook her head. "No, I have the pistol. You keep that with you and keep it safe."

The boy nodded solemnly, slung the rifle on his shoulder and moved toward Derek's side, where he grabbed ahold of Derek's jacket near the hem. "I'll take good care of him, Aunt Flynn."

"You need my help," Derek protested. He took a step in her direction, but Kevin pulled him back and Flynn held up her hands in a motion to stop him.

"Please, do what I'm asking," she said softly. She quickly pulled off her gloves and tossed them aside, then gently caressed Derek's cheek. His skin was pale from blood loss and pain, and she hated to rush off and leave him behind, but she had no choice. She had to stop Adam Cary, and she also had to make sure Kevin was protected. "Please. You're injured. Stay with Kevin and keep him safe. You're the only one I can trust. And while you're at it, get some medical help for that shoulder." She dropped her hand and took a step back toward the front hospital door, then turned and ran, unzipping her pocket as she went so she would have easy access to the pistol.

She could feel Derek's eyes on her and knew he wasn't happy about being left behind, but it had to be done. Derek and Kevin were the two most important men in her life right now, and she needed them both out of harm's way while she confronted Adam Cary.

She quickly made it to the front entrance and passed the lobby kiosk, her eyes surveying the room, looking for any signs of Cary or his minions. She saw neither and ignored the stares and questions from the staff at the help desk. Finally, the lit sign for the stairwell caught her eye, and she ran to the entryway and rushed up the steps. The last time she had visited Erin, her sister had been on the third floor in the ICU department. Adam Cary had undoubtedly taken the elevator. She didn't have a moment to lose.

Her breath caught in her chest as she reached the top floor. She pulled her pistol, verified the safety was off and a bullet was in the chamber, and pointed the weapon toward the floor. She took a moment to get her bearings, then rushed to the nurses' station. She didn't see Cary, or anyone moving around in the halls, for that matter, but he had to be close. There was a nurse leaning over a computer keyboard at the desk, and she quickly tried to get her attention. "I'm here to see Erin Denning. She's in danger…"

Something wasn't right. The nurse was actually lying on the keyboard and wasn't moving. Flynn reached over the counter, touched her shoulder and tried to shake her, and in response, the woman's body leaned to the left and then slowly fell out of the chair. Blood covered the front of her scrubs where a bullet had recently ended her life, and a pool of blood had formed on and under the keyboard and was dripping silently onto the floor. The poor woman's face still showed her surprise.

Panic swamped over Flynn. Assuming a law enforcement stance, she continued to point her pistol at the floor and moved as quietly as possible toward the room where her sister had been the last time she visited. Was Erin already dead?

Dread and fear tightened a knot in her stomach as she cautiously approached the room. She inched past the door and peeked quickly through the glass wall that separated the room from the hallway.

There was no one in the bed. In fact, the bare mattress was sitting on the bedframe without sheets or pillows, as if the room had been unoccupied for some time. There were no machines, no tubes or monitors, and no notes on the dry-erase board that previously listed the patient's name, medical condition and when she had last received her medication.

A dread she hadn't prepared for physically made her stomach twist even tighter, and the pain hurt so badly that she almost sank to the floor. Grief and heartache melted together and nearly incapacitated her. Had Erin died while they'd been fighting their way down the mountain today, or had it been while they'd been sleeping in the snow cave? Had she been alone at the final hour, or had someone been with her to hold her hand? Regret mixed in with the other emotions and began to take precedence. Flynn had never had a chance to say goodbye or tell her sister how much she loved her. Now, she would never get that chance. She couldn't believe her sister had died, and yet the bed was definitely empty, and her sister's body was nowhere around.

A scream behind her surprised her, and she turned quickly and aimed at the newcomer, her hands amazingly steady despite the sentiments running rampant in her body.

A young female health-care assistant carrying a stack of clean sheets and towels had just come across the dead woman at the nurses' station, and her shrieks grew louder as Flynn approached. When she saw the gun in Flynn's hand, she dropped the linens and took several steps back, obviously terrified and thinking Flynn was the shooter. She held up her hands in a motion of surrender. "Don't kill me, too! Please!"

"I didn't shoot her," Flynn said, keeping her tone as calm as possible. She lowered the weapon. "But I'm a cop and I'm looking for the man who did. He's tall, has dark hair and eyes, and is wearing a black overcoat. Have you seen him? I'm pretty sure he was just here."

The woman stopped whimpering but shook her head. She took another step back, as if she wasn't quite sure whether she should believe Flynn or not.

"He wants to hurt my sister, Erin Denning, who was in room 342 a couple of days ago. Do you know what happened to her?"

The orderly's breath was coming fast, but she pulled herself together and moved over to the desk behind the counter, trying her best not to look at the dead woman's body as she grabbed a clipboard off the wall. Flynn didn't have a badge to show her, but the orderly was either too scared to ask or unconcerned about her lack of credentials. Or maybe she remembered Flynn visiting Erin for several days and seeing her around the hospital. Regardless, Flynn was happy that the young woman was ready and willing to help her out, especially when every second mattered. "Erin Denning got better and they moved her to a different room." She flipped through a couple of pages. "Here she is—room 267."

"Thanks," Flynn said, already heading toward the stairs. She leaped down them two at a time and burst through the door onto the second floor, then eyed the directory and took the hallway to the right.

Chaos reigned. She slowed as she passed the nursing station and stopped completely as she took in the scene. Hospital personnel were huddled behind furniture and computer carts and peeking around at the showdown that was happening in the hallway.

About thirty feet away, Adam Cary was standing in the hallway. He was still dressed the same as he'd been up on the mountain with his fancy suit and topcoat, and he looked oddly out of place in the hospital, as if he'd just come from a board meeting or a face-to-face appointment with an attorney.

He also had Erin Denning by the neck and held a

9mm handgun with a silencer pressed against her temple. Erin was very much alive but still weak and pale. Despite her current circumstance, however, Erin's eyes locked with Flynn's, and Flynn could see her sister's fighting spirit was still very much alive and well.

Flynn's emotions were already near a breaking point, but when she saw the danger her sister was in, a new wave of both relief and fear swamped her as she quickly stepped to the left and took cover behind a cart holding several trays of food. Her sister was alive! Not only that, but she was conscious. Flynn's heart squeezed, and she felt her stomach twist even tighter, like she was on a roller coaster. She remembered quite vividly how her sister had been in a coma when she'd left the hospital a few days ago. Erin's eyes were vibrant now, but it was also painfully obvious that she was still very ill. She was definitely not well enough to be dragged out into the hall by a madman and was struggling to stand, yet she also didn't have much choice. Cary's grip was firm, and he had a ghost of a smile on his face, as if he was pleased with the control he wielded, despite the circumstances. Flynn had missed the drama that had preceded this event and wasn't exactly sure what all had happened, but in the grand scheme of things, all that really mattered was her sister's life.

"Mr. Cary, you don't need to hurt her," Flynn called out. "Just tell us what you want and we'll help you get out of here."

"Nice try," he replied, his voice all business as if he was discussing his company's quarterly earning reports. "This woman is my get-out-of-jail-free card."

Flynn was an excellent shot. She'd made a name for

herself in her agency as one of the best sharpshooters ever seen in her department. But shooting at a target and shooting at a madman who was holding her only sister hostage were two entirely different things. She loved her sister with all her heart. What if she missed? What if Adam Cary moved at the last second and Erin became the target? What if she hit Erin by mistake? She looked at the pistol in her grip and noticed that her hands were shaking. It was impossible to be accurate with any weapon if she couldn't steady herself and carefully squeeze the trigger. This was her sister's life! How could she live with herself if she killed or injured her?

Yet how could she let this drug dealer drag Erin out of the hospital? If Adam Cary managed to get her out the door and into a vehicle of any kind, he would definitely kill her sister as soon as he no longer needed her. Also, if Flynn didn't stop Cary here and now, the man would grow his drug enterprise and continue to leave a path of destruction in his wake as the poison he sold desecrated the lives of everyone around him. He had enough money to buy the best and brightest attorneys, who could probably even manage to somehow get him off for the poor murdered nurse whose body was still warm on the floor above them.

She locked eyes with her sister, whose expression was one of fear and trepidation, yet she could also see hope in those brown depths.

What should she do?

Derek couldn't handle letting Flynn confront Adam Cary by himself. Even injured and unsure if he could help or not, it just was not in him to stay behind. He had no clear plan in mind besides protecting Flynn and keeping her safe. That was his one and only goal. He left Kevin and the rifle with the security guard at the emergency room entrance with little explanation, but promised to return shortly and ran out to the front of the hospital and raced through the automatic glass doors. He headed straight to the stairwell, and just as he entered, he heard her coming back down the stairs in a rush. He stepped back against the wall on the level below her to avoid the confrontation, and she didn't notice him as she charged down to the second floor. Mere seconds behind her, he surreptitiously entered the floor and took in the scene. Instantly he analyzed the situation, and the angst in Flynn's body language and expression as she noticed him from her refuge behind the tray cart and acknowledged him with a nod.

He didn't have two good arms, but he did have something she didn't have—an idea of the general setup of the hospital. He'd been here several times before while visiting an old friend who was getting cancer treatments on this very floor. It had been a year or so since he'd been here, but it was a small hospital, and he felt confident there had been little change, if any, to the general layout. He made a motion to Flynn to wait, then turned and took the stairs back down to the first floor, ignored the guard who was yelling at him to return to the emergency room and get the boy, and headed for the second set of stairs that would come out behind where Adam Cary was holding Erin. He reached the stairway door and stopped, surprised to see a lit keypad by the door lock. He knew the stairs were used by doctors and hospital staff and were not meant for the general public, but they hadn't been locked before. He pulled on the door, just in case, but verified that the red light did indeed mean the door was firmly locked. He looked around desperately and saw the security guard approaching with Kevin in tow.

"Look, fella," he said testily. "I ain't no babysitting service. You've got to take the kid with you. And you should know better than to leave a weapon like this in the hands of a kid." He shook the rifle. "Hospitals are no place for guns, buddy. I can't do my job with you just leaving him—"

"I need your key card for the stairs," Derek demanded. "There's a man on the second floor holding a gun on a patient. I need to get up there to help."

The guard's eyebrows lifted. "Are you serious?"

"Is that my mom?" Kevin asked at the same time.

"Yes," Derek answered both questions at the same time.

"Well, I can't just give you—" the guard started.

He didn't get a chance to finish. The guard had the credit card–size badge attached to a retractable holder that snapped on his belt, and Kevin noticed, yanked it off and thrust it into Derek's good right hand. "Save my mom!" Kevin pleaded.

The guard made a grab for the key card, but Kevin swiftly blocked the man and pushed him back. Once Derek had the card, he quickly used it to open the door, then pocketed it in case he needed it again.

The guard continued to protest, but Derek gave him a withering look, and the smaller man backed up and held up his hands. "I'm calling the police," the guard threatened with narrowed eyes.

"You do that, but keep an eye on the boy in the meantime," Derek said fiercely. "If anything happens to him,

I'm coming after you next." He paused on the stairs. "And tell them to bring a body bag for the bad guy." He took one last moment to lock eyes with Kevin, and he gave the boy a reassuring smile. "Stay here. I promise I'll do everything I can to save her." He turned back to the stairs, letting the door close softly behind him.

Could he make it to the scene and do something—anything—to help Flynn before it was too late? His injured shoulder and arm were a problem. He couldn't shoot a rifle with one arm, and he didn't have any other weapon. Still, he had to try.

With his heart beating like a bass drum, he ran up the stairs.

NINETEEN

Four bullets. Flynn checked the clip again, just to verify her ammunition. Yep. That's all she had left. Three in the magazine and one in the chamber. It would have to be enough.

"Let Erin go," she demanded, her tone firm as she called out to Cary. "Nobody's going to stop you if you try to walk out of here. She'll just slow you down."

"You're right nobody is going to stop me. This woman is my insurance plan. Now, everybody back up or I'll shoot her right here and now." Cary's voice was vicious and confident and held the air of authority that came from running a criminal enterprise and never having his orders questioned. He probably believed he would escape unscathed and his army of lawyers could fix any mess he left behind. His arrogance was irritating.

She heard Erin whimper and glanced around the cart. Cary had pulled Erin even tighter against him and was moving toward her. Her mind reeled. How could she stop him without putting her sister's life in jeopardy?

Flynn knew one thing—Adam Cary was not leaving this hospital with Erin in tow. She made that decision, even though she still had no idea how she was going to stop him. If Cary managed to get Erin alone somewhere, her sister was as good as dead. He would surely kill her once she was no longer necessary for his escape. Flynn said a silent prayer, then took a deep, calming breath once she finished. God was with her. She could feel a peace invade her chest that hadn't been there moments before. *I will never leave thee nor forsake thee.* The Bible verse came instantly to mind and gave her another measure of peace. Unbidden, another verse also floated into her heart. *I can do all things through Christ which stregtheneth me.* She stepped out from behind the cart and pointed the gun at Adam Cary's head—at least the part of it she could see.

"I changed my mind. I am going to stop you. You're under arrest, Adam Cary, and you're not taking my sister anywhere." Her voice held all the steel she could muster.

She heard murmurs behind her from hospital staff, but she tuned everything out—everything except the eyes of the man holding her sister at gunpoint.

He smiled at her audacity. "I'm holding the life of your sister in my hand. Are you really going to challenge me?" His voice was filled with derision, as if he considered her threat completely inconsequential. He probably had good reason. He was a powerful man, with not only wealth at his disposal but also an arsenal of armed men that constituted his own private army. For all she knew, he had people just waiting to shoot her the moment she left the building. She thought back to the many men who had been chasing them over the last few days and the fate of Lee Clark. Yes, Adam Cary was undoubtedly very formidable and rarely got challenged. But this was her sister. Flynn would sacrifice whatever it took to free her from the man's grasp—even her own life.

Suddenly, several things happened in the blink of an eye. A loud bang sounded behind Cary and her sister, as if an entire computer cart had been upended and thrown across the floor. Within seconds of hearing the sound, Erin elbowed Cary hard when he took a distracted moment to turn and see what was going on behind him. As a result, he relaxed his hold on her neck, and she pulled against his arm, throwing him off balance.

That moment was all Flynn needed. She aimed, steadied her breathing and squeezed the trigger.

Time suddenly seemed to go into slow motion.

The bullet caught Adam Cary in the forehead, and his body was pushed back by the force of the blow. His arms fell away from his captive, and he crumpled to the floor, his gun landing on the ground and skittering away. Erin pushed away from him and took several steps away before leaning heavily on a small linen cart that was a few feet away. Her hospital gown was twisted around her legs, but she didn't seem to care as relief painted her features.

As Cary fell and Erin moved, Flynn could plainly see Derek standing behind them but to the side, safely out of the trajectory of her bullet.

Derek was in pain and injured and only had one arm he could use, but he had used what he could to cause the distraction she needed to gain the upper hand. He gave her a nod, then turned and disappeared back into the stairwell as she rushed forward and enveloped Erin in a bear hug.

"Oh, thank God!" Flynn said vehemently. "I'm so glad you're alive!"

* * *

"Ouch." Derek flinched a short time later as he sat on the edge of the bed in the emergency room where they'd taken him after the chaos had started to settle down. He'd immediately returned to the first floor and found Kevin, then brought the boy back up to his mother in her hospital room on the second floor. Flynn, Erin and Kevin had had a tearful reunion, and he had unobtrusively stepped back out, leaving the family to celebrate their survival. It had only taken Flynn a few minutes, though, to realize he had gone and to search and find him in the seats down by the nurses' station. She had enveloped him in the warmest hug he'd ever received and then walked him back to the emergency room for his exam. He would have made it there himself eventually, but exhaustion and relief had caught up to him first and he had taken a few minutes to just sit and regroup.

They had survived. Their journey was finally over. A prayer of thankfulness was in order, and he had done just that, right there by the elevators with Flynn in his arms.

It hadn't taken the police long to arrive, and in between medical exams, he and Flynn had explained the entire story, starting with the coordinates that Erin had discovered during her initial investigation and how they had flown up to see the site. Flynn had produced the SD card from her boot, and the detectives had taken it quickly, excited to see the photos that documented the murdered dealers and would undoubtedly bolster their case. They assured her that if the photos showed what she promised, they would have no problem using them to investigate the drug cartel and dismantle it piece by piece.

The doctor raised an eyebrow at Derek's complaint but made a slight adjustment. "You've had the local anesthesia. It should have numbed the area so I can stitch you up."

"I feel like a giant pincushion."

The doctor laughed. "You should be glad that we didn't have to surgically repair that shoulder."

"I'll take your word for it," Derek said as he winced again. "I hate hospitals."

"He's a big baby," Flynn laughed, and her smile grew as Derek furrowed his brow, then winked at her.

"Let him stick a needle in you and see how you like it," Derek muttered, although his tone was playful and contradicted his stormy words. After X-rays and a thorough examination, the emergency room doctor had pulled out a suture kit and begun the work of closing the wound. Although Derek would need some physical therapy after the wound healed, the doctor was confident his patient would regain full use of his arm.

Flynn grabbed his good hand and gave it a squeeze, and then to Derek's surprise, she didn't let it go. She was touching him and not pulling away. "Thank you for causing that distraction in the hallway. I was worried about my aim. You gave me the extra help I needed." She pulled his hand up to her lips and brushed his knuckles against her lips, and he reveled at their softness. Had her feelings for him returned? He saw a glow in her eyes and hoped it was the same love that was slowly spreading and warming his chest. The doctor finished up, picked up his tray and let them know a nurse would be by soon to start the discharge process. Once they were alone, Derek took a chance, laying all his cards face up on the table. He met Flynn's eye and gave her a tender smile.

"You know, we've been through a lot the last couple of days. It's amazing how much a person can learn in just a short time."

She raised an eyebrow and quirked her lips. "Oh, really? And what have you learned?"

He tilted his head. "I've learned to put the past behind me, and that I need God in my life." He reached for her hand, squeezed her fingers, then released her. "I also need you." He took his good hand and gently cupped the back of her head and drew her near for a kiss. She came closer willingly, her hesitance slowly receding, and the kiss was soft and sweet and full of promise. When they finally drew apart, he pulled her close again into a bear hug embrace with his good arm. This time she didn't stiffen in his arms but instead molded against him. Holding her felt so right. He didn't want to ever let her go.

"I was so wrong to leave you after graduation—really, really wrong." He pulled back a bit, but only so he could see into her eyes. "Marry me, Flynn Denning? I love you with all my heart. I can't go on without you. Please say you'll be my wife."

Flynn took her hand and drew it slowly down his cheek, then kissed him again. It was even better than the first, and full of promise. "Yes, I'll marry you, Derek. I never stopped loving you. Never."

EPILOGUE

"And now, ladies and gentlemen, we'd like to award our three heroes a key to our wonderful town of Frisco, Colorado. As you know, the key to the city is a beloved symbol of civic recognition and gratitude, which is reserved for individuals whose service to the public and the common good rises to the highest level of achievement. Derek and Flynn King, and Kevin Wallace, are being awarded this key because of their outstanding work in putting the largest drug cartel in Colorado's history out of business. Not only is Frisco, Colorado, a safer city to live in today because of their efforts, but indeed, the entire state of Colorado has benefited from their work, and we thank them from the bottom of our hearts."

The mayor gave an award box to each of them, and they opened them together. Each had a golden key inscribed with their names and the date with *Frisco, Colorado*, embroidered into the box lining. They were beautiful awards but made Flynn a little uncomfortable. After all, they would have done their best to stop the drug dealers regardless and didn't need an award for their efforts. Still, the mayor and town council had been quite insistent, and she and Derek had finally acquiesced.

Flynn looked over at her sister, Erin, who was standing a few feet away, almost completely healed from her ordeal almost six months ago. During that time, she had shared everything she had discovered about Bear Creek Vacation Rentals with her team at the local police department. Due to her diligence and efforts, the photos that Flynn had managed to salvage, the driver's license of the other murder victim that Derek had saved and all their eyewitness testimony, the Frisco police had been able to cripple the drug cartel and make dozens of arrests. The mayor had wanted to give Erin a key to the city as well, but she had refused in no uncertain terms. She was a police officer, and weeding out crime was her duty. Besides, she claimed Flynn, Derek and Kevin had done the heavy lifting by actually finding the meth lab and escaping down the mountain to bring the drug dealers to justice.

Flynn smiled over at Derek and then slipped into his arms as the crowd slowly dispersed. He gave her a gentle squeeze, then took her hand. They had been married about two months ago and she couldn't be happier. It had been hard for her to learn to trust again, but after all the difficulties they'd faced together on the mountain, she had realized that being together with Derek was just where she wanted and needed to be. They had both welcomed God back into their lives, and over the past few months, they had grown closer and loved each other more than she ever thought possible.

She turned and smiled at Kevin, who had rushed over to his mom and was showing her his award. He was very proud of the golden key, as well he should be. He had lived with Flynn for about two months before the wedding, and

she had been able to get him in with a Christian coun-
selor, who had really been helping him sort through his
feelings. Derek had also played a large role in the boy's
healing as well and been spending quite a bit of quality
time with him. The time Derek had spent had been ca-
thartic for Derek as well, and she had been amazed to
see the change in him around Kevin. Their relationship
was exciting to witness as they helped each other grow.

She glanced over at her sister. Erin had been able to
come home with the help of a home health aide, whose
services had eventually become unnecessary as she had
regained her strength. She was now almost back to one
hundred percent and had returned to desk duty on the
police force. She claimed she was ready to hit the streets
again as soon as the doctors gave her a release, which
she expected any day, but Flynn was glad Erin's supe-
riors were taking it slowly. She knew Erin could handle
herself, but she wanted her sister to be as strong as possible before going back onto regular duty.

"Pretty exciting day," Derek said softly as they walked
hand in hand back toward their vehicle. "It sure is great
the way you've been welcomed here in Frisco." He
stopped for a minute so he could read her expression
better. "What did you decide to do about the mayor's
job offer?"

Flynn had given up her job in Florida when she'd
moved to Colorado and married him, and although he
was delighted and excited to have her sharing his life,
he knew she had sacrificed a lot by leaving her job and
friends behind. Thankfully, the governor had pulled
some strings and gotten her a job offer from the local

Border Patrol office, but she hadn't officially accepted yet. Derek hadn't even realized the Border Patrol had a representative in the area, but if that's what Flynn wanted to do, then he would support her choice.

"I'm not sure yet," she murmured. "I'll probably end up taking it in nine months or so." She smiled and changed the subject. "I love the way you and Kevin have been doing so much together. Erin and I have both seen a huge improvement in his behavior, and it's largely due to your efforts. Thank you."

Derek shrugged. "He's a great kid. You know, I was always scared of being a father. That's the whole reason why I ran away to the army in the first place. But after getting to know Kevin, I've realized I don't have to be like my father. I think I would be a good dad someday."

Flynn leaned forward and kissed him. There was a sweet smile on her face that told him there was more to come, and he laughed. "What?"

"I'm just really glad to hear you say that," she said with a mischievous look in her eye. "I'm pregnant."

* * * * *

Available now from Love Inspired Suspense!

Find more great reads at www.LoveInspired.com.

Dear Reader,

In John 16:33, the Bible clearly tells us that we will struggle in life, yet, in Deuteronomy 31:8, the Lord also promises that He will never leave us nor forsake us. He goes through the tough times with us, cries when we cry, and hurts when we hurt. If you are walking through a difficult situation, take heart. You are not alone. Jesus loves you and is right by your side. Lean on Him. Be thankful for the good in your life, and remember, spring is coming.

Thank you for reading my book! I truly appreciate you.

May God bless you!
Kathleen Tailer

HARLEQUIN
Reader Service

Enjoyed your book?

Try the perfect subscription for Romance readers and get more great books like this delivered right to your door.

See why over 10+ million readers have tried Harlequin Reader Service.

Start with a Free Welcome Collection with free books and a gift—valued over $20.

Choose any series in print or ebook.
See website for details and order today:

TryReaderService.com/subscriptions